Biblioasis International
General Editor: Stephen Henighan

RAIN AND OTHER STORIES

Rain and Other Stories

Mia Couto

Translated from the Portuguese by
Eric M. B. Becker

BIBLIOASIS
WINDSOR, ONTARIO

Originally published as *Estórias Abensonhadas: Contos* by Editorial Caminho, Lisbon, Portugal, 1994.

FIRST EDITION

Library and Archives Canada Cataloguing in Publication

Couto, Mia, 1955-
[Short stories. Selections. English]
      Rain & other stories / Mia Couto ; translated from the Portuguese by Eric M. B. Becker.

(Biblioasis international translation series ; 25)
Issued in print and electronic formats.
ISBN 978-1-77196-266-7 (softcover).—ISBN 978-1-77196-267-4 (ebook)

      1. Couto, Mia, 1955- —Translations into English. I. Becker, Eric M. B., translator II. Title. III. Series: Biblioasis international translation series ; no. 25

Edited by Stephen Henighan, Daniel Wells, and David Brookshaw
Copy-edited by Jessica Faulds
Typeset by Chris Andrechek
Cover designed by Zoe Norvell

Funded by the Direção-Geral do Livro, dos Arquivos e das Bibliotecas.

PRINTED AND BOUND IN CANADA

Contents

These tales were written after the war. For years without end, gun-fire had spilled mourning all across Mozambique. These stories came to me between the banks of anguish and hope. After the war, I thought all that was left was ashes, hollow ruins. Everything weighing on me, definitive and without repair.

Today, I know that's not true. Where man remains, a seed, too, survives, a dream to inseminate time. This dream hid in the most inaccessible parts of us, in the space where violence could not strike, where barbarism could not enter. During all this time, the earth protected, intact, its voices. When silence was imposed on them, the voices shifted worlds. In the dark, they remained lunar.

The tales here speak of this land we are remaking and where we soak our faces in this rain of hope, this water of benedreamtion. Of this land where each man is the same, like this: pretending he's here, dreaming of going away, imagining his return.

The Waters of Time

My grandfather, in those days, would take me down the river, tucked into the tiny canoe he called a *concho*. He would row, lazurely, barely scraping the oar across the current. The little boat bobbled, wave here, wave there, lonelier, it seemed, than a fallen, forgotten tree trunk.

—*But where are you two going?*

That was my mother's torment. The old man would smile. Teeth, in his case, were an indefinite article. Grandpa was one of those men who are silent in their knowing and converse without really saying a thing.

—*We'll be back in no time,* he would respond.

Not even I knew what he was pursuing. It wasn't fish. The net remained in place, cushioning the seat. It was a guarantee that when the unappointed hour arrived, the day already twilighting, he would grip my hand and pull me toward the bank. He held me like a blind man. All the same, it was he who guided me, one step ahead of me. I was astonished at his upright gauntness, all of him musclyboned. Grandfather was a man in full-fledged childhood, perpetually enraptured by the novelty of living.

We would climb into the boat, our feet a stroke on the belly of a drum. The canoe pulleyed, drowned in dreams. Before leaving, the old man would lean over one of the sides and gather up a bit of water with a cupped hand. I imitated him.

—Always with the water, never forget!

That was his constant warning. Drawing water against the current could bring misfortune. The flowing spirits won't be contradicted.

Later, we'd travel as far as the large lake into which our tiny river emptied. That was the realm of forbidden creatures. All that showed itself there, after all, invented its existence. In that place, the boundary between water and earth disappeared. In the unquiet calm, atop the lily-rippled waters, we were the only ones who prevailed. Our tiny boat floated in place, dozing to the gentle lull. Grandfather, hushed, observed the distant banks. Everything around us bathed in cool breezes, shadows made of light itself, as if the morning were eternally drowned in dreams. We would sit there as if in prayer, so quiet as to appear perfect.

Then my grandfather would suddenly stand in the *concho*. With the rocking, the boat nearly tossed us out. The old man, excited, would wave. He'd take out his red cloth and shake it decisively. Whom was he signalling? Maybe it was no one.

At no point, not even for an instant, did I glimpse a soul from this or any other world. But my grandfather would continue to wave his cloth.

—*Don't you see it, there on the bank? Behind the mist?*

I didn't see it. But he would insist, unbuttoning his nerves.

—*It's not there. It's theeeere. Don't you see the white cloth, dancing?*

All I saw was a heavy fog before us and the frightful beyond, where the horizon disappeared. My elder, later on, would lose sight of the mirage and withdraw, shrunken in his silence. And then we would return, travelling without the company of words.

At home, my mother would greet us sourly. Soon she would forbid me from doing many things. She didn't want us going to the lake, she feared the dangers that lurked there. First she would become angry with my grandfather, suspicious of his non-intentions. But afterward, already softened by our arrival, she would test out a joke:

—*You could at least have spotted the* namwetxo moha! *Then, at least, we'd have the benefit of some good luck…*

The *namwetxo moha* was a spirit that emerged at night, made only of halves: one eye, one leg, one arm. We were children, and adventurous, and we'd go out looking for the *moha*. But we never found any such creature. My grandfather would belittle us. He'd say that, when still a youth, he'd come face to face with this certain half-fellow. An invention of his own mind, my mother would warn. But, being mere children, we had no desire to doubt him.

One time, at the forbidden lake, Grandpa and I waited for the habitual emergence of the cloths. We were on the bank where the greens become reeds, enfluted. They say: the first man was born of these reeds. The first man? For me, there couldn't be any man more ancient than my grandfather. It so happened that, on this occasion, I hungered to see the marshes. I wanted to climb the bank, set foot on unsolid ground.

—Never! Never do that!

He spoke in the gravest of tones. I had never seen my elder look so possessed. I apologized: I was getting off the boat, but only for a little while. Then he retorted:

—In this place, there aren't any little whiles. All time, from here on out, is eternity.

I had a foot half out of the boat, seeking the boggy floor of the bank. I sought to steady myself. I looked for ground where I could put my foot down. It happened that I found no bottom— my leg kept falling, swallowed by the abyss. The old man rushed to my aid and pulled me back toward the boat. But the force sucking me downward was greater than our effort. With the commotion, the boat overturned and we fell backwards into the water. And so we were stuck there, struggling in the lake, clinging to the sides of the canoe. Suddenly, my grandfather pulled his cloth from the boat and began to wave it above his head.

—Go on, you greet him too!

I looked toward the bank but saw no one. But I obeyed my grandpa, waving without conviction. Then something astonishing happened: all of a sudden, we stopped being pulled into the depths. The whirlpool that had seized us vanished in an immediate calm. We returned to the boat and sighed in shared relief. In silence, we split the work of the return voyage. As he tied up the boat, the old man told me:

—*Don't say a word about what happened. Not even to no one, you hear?*

That night, he explained his reasons. My ears opened wide to decipher his hoarse voice. I couldn't understand it all. He said, more or less: *We have eyes that open to the inside, these we use to see our dreams. It so happens, my boy, that nearly all are blind, they no longer see those others who visit us. Others, you ask? Yes, those who wave to us from the other bank. And so we provoke their complete sadness. I take you there to the marshes so you might learn to see. I must not be the last to be visited by the cloths.*

—*Understand me?*

I lied and said that I did. The following afternoon, my grandfather took me once more to the lake. Arriving at the edge of dusk, he sat there watching. But time passed with unusual sloth. My grandfather grew anxious, propped on the boat's bow, the palm of his hand refining the view. On the other side there was less than no one. This time, my grandfather, too, saw nothing more than the misty solitude of the marshes. Suddenly, he interrupted the nothing:

—Wait here!

And he jumped to the bank as fear stole my breath. Was my grandfather stepping into the forbidden country? Yes. In the face of my shock, he kept walking with confident steps. The canoe wobbled in disequilibrium with my off-balance weight. I witnessed the old man distancing himself with the discretion of a cloud. Until, enveloped in mist, he sank into dream, at the margin of the mirage. I stood there, in shock, trembling in the shivering cold. I recall seeing an enormous white egret cut across the sky. It looked like an arrow piercing the flanks of the afternoon, making all the firmament bleed. It was then I beheld on the bank, from the other side of the world, the white cloth. For the first time, I saw the cloth as my grandfather had. Even as I doubted what I saw, there, right alongside the apparition, was my grandfather's red cloth, still waving. I hesitated, disordered. Then, slowly, I removed my shirt and shook it in the air. I saw the red of his cloth becoming white, its colour fading. My eyes misted until the visions became dusk.

As I rowed a long return, the old words of my old grandfather came to mind: water and time are twin brothers, born of the same womb. I had just discovered in myself a river that would never die. It's to that river I now return, guiding my son, teaching him to glimpse the white cloths on the other bank.

Novidade's Flowers

Novidade Castigo was the daughter of Veronica Manga and the miner Jonasse Nhamitando. She gained the nickname Castigo because, true to the moniker, she came into the world like a punishment. That much could be surmised shortly after her birth, from the blue that shone in her eyes. A black girl, the daughter of black parents: Where had this blue come from?

Let's begin with the girl: she was astonishingly beautiful, with a face to incur the envy of angels. Not even water was more pristine. Her one drawback, though: she was slow in the head, her thoughts never seemed to stay the night. She'd become that way—amiss—when one day, already a young woman, she suffered a fit of convulsions. That night, Veronica was sitting on the veranda when she felt insomnia's spider-crawl across her chest.

—*Tonight I'm going to count stars*, she predicted.

The night was already biting its fingernails toward dawn when, in one corner of the house, the young girl awoke in spasms and convulsions, as though her flesh were trying to break free from her soul. Her mother, predicting the future from the shadows, sensed a muted warning: What had happened? Light as a fright, she ran to young Novidade's bedside. In the houses of the poor all is well according to the degree of tidiness or disarray. Veronica Manga cut through the dark, dodged crates and cans, leapt over hoes and sacks, until she drew closer to her daughter and saw her arm, hoisted like a flag drooping at full-mast. Veronica didn't call for Novidade's father. It wasn't worth interrupting his rest.

Only the next morning did she relate what had happened. Jonasse was preparing to take off for his job on the eve of his descent into the belly of the mountain. He stopped at the door, reconsidering his intentions. Jonasse Nhamitando, all father-like, went to his daughter's room and found her lying still, her only wish to rest. Without removing his rough, worn glove, he tenderly stroked her face. Was he saying goodbye to another girl, the one who had been his little daughter? Then, the young girl's father left the way a cloud parts from the rain.

The years passed in less than a blink of an eye. Novidade grew up, nothing new there. Her parents had acknowledged and assented to the idea: their daughter had sealed Veronica's womb. She wasn't an only child: she was a none-ly child, a creature of singular stock. Jonasse was a kind man, he refused to abandon Veronica. And the couple's daughter, in a pact with the void, showered her father with love and tenderness. Not that she put this into words. Rather, she did so by the way she would wait, suspended in time, for the miner's return home. For the duration of each of the miner's shifts, the girl remained apprehensive, neither eating nor drinking. Only after the father returned would the girl reassume her normal expression, and, in her voice like a stream, they discovered tunes that no one, save the girl, knew. And then there were the gifts she would pick for him: bizarre little flowers of no other colour than the blue found in her eyes. No one ever learned where she plucked such petals.

Many nights later, the family relived their earlier suffering. Jonasse was nowhere to be found. The miner was out digging the earth full of holes on the night shift. Back at the house, his wife's eyes rested over the rim of the light coming from the *xipefo*, as they called the oil lamp. She stitched together swaddlings of nothing, tiny clothes for a son who, as they well knew, would never come. Little Novidade dozed at the woman's side. The girl began to curl up, convulsing, her epilepsy an epic lapse. Her mother quickly tended to her. In her panic, she shattered the light to pieces, overturning the gas lamp and its glowing light. As she calmed the girl, who was all lips and heavy breathing, Veronica Manga sought the matches above the chest. Only then did a muddy sound from the mountain outside call her attention. What was that? The mine exploding? Good heavens! She broke out in goosebumps. And Jonasse, her husband?

The woman zigzagged through the house in a run-or-die, moved from anxiety to alarm, a fly in a bull's tail. And then came even bigger explosions. Seen from the window, the mountain was transformed into a fire-breathing pangolin. Would boulders and bedrock tumble down upon the houses? No, the mountain, that one at least, had a tough constitution. And what about Jonasse? The woman knew she would have to wait till morning for news of her husband. But the young girl didn't wait for the morning light. In silence, she gathered up her tiny things in a basket and a sack. Then she arranged her mother's belongings in an old suitcase. Finally a few meagre words, in a gentle command, came from her mouth.

—*Let's go, Mother!*

Without stopping to think, the girl's mother abandoned her post, the spot where she'd nested for so many years. She let the young girl lead her by the hand, trusting in who knows what intuition. Along the way, the two of them crossed some others, like them, on the run. And Veronica asked them:

—*This thing we're hearing: What is it?*

It wasn't coming from the mine. Those were military explosions, the war was approaching. *And our husbands, where can they go to save themselves?*

—*There's no time. Climb onto the truck,* the others responded.

And up they went. Veronica situated her things better than herself, and made Novidade sit on top of the basket. The motor turned over, spinning more slowly than her eyes in their anxious search to find Jonasse emerging from the clouds of smoke and chaos. The truck pulled away, leaving behind only debris and explosions. Mother stood looking at her daughter, the composure in her expression, her dirty dress. What was she doing? Humming. In the midst of that whirlwind, the girl panned for bits of joy amid her quiet songs. Was she defanging that moment pregnant with disaster?

Between bombs and gunshots, the truck pulled forward until it reached the front of the mine where Jonasse worked. And then the girl, disregarding the moment's developments, leapt to the ill-advised ground. She took a few steps forward, ironing out the wrinkles in her little dress, turned backward to offer her mother a sign of affection. Horrified, the vehicle came to a halt. Little Novidade resumed her path, crossing the road exposed to certain danger. The truck honked its horn in fury: the only thing that took its time there was death. The girl didn't appear to even hear. She stood in the road as if the way were entirely hers. In the dictionary of her footsteps, there was no sign of arrogance, nor any grand declarations. The fact that she was standing in the road, upsetting the chaos, wasn't an act of defiance but of distraction, plain and simple. She put the blue of her eyes to use. The driver, all nerves, called for her one last time. And the rest of the passengers screamed for her mother to order her to return. But Veronica didn't utter a word.

Atop a pile of sand pulled from the mine, Little Novidade leaned down to pluck wildflowers, the kind one spots on roadsides. She chose them at a cemetery pace. She stopped before some tiny blue petals, identical to the colour of her eyes. The truck, tired of waiting, beset by the distressed clamour of its passengers, darted down the road. The mother refused to look away from her daughter, as though she wished to see her fate in its final form. What happened next, no one knows. Only she could see it. There, amid the dust: what happened was the flowers, the ones with a blue glimmer, began to swell and soar toward the sky. Then, all together, they plucked the girl. The flowers grabbed hold of Little Novidade with their petals and pulled her down into the earth. The girl seemed to expect this, as, smiling, she was swept away into the same womb where she'd seen her father extinguished, out of sight and out of time.

Blind Estrelinho

Blind Estrelinho was a man of no moment: were it not for his guide, Gigito Efraim, his story could be recounted and discounted. Gigito's hand had led the unvisioned man for ages and ages. That hand was separate yet shared, an extension of one man into the other, siamesely. And so it had been almost from birth. Estrelinho's memory had five fingers and they were those of Gigito, gripped firmly in his own hand.

The blind man, curious, wanted to know everything. He didn't make a fuss about life. For him, always was too seldom and everything insufficient. He would say, with these words:

—*I've got to live right away, or else I'll forget.*

Little Gigito, however—he described what wasn't there. The world he detailed was fantasies and fine-lacery. The guide's imagination bore more fruit than a papaya tree. The blind man's mouth filled with waters:

—*What marvellosity, this world. Tell me everything, Gigito!*

The guide's hand was, after all, a manuscript of lies. Gigito Efraim was as Saint Thomas never had been: he saw to not believe. The aide spoke through his fingertips. He peeled open the universe, abloom in petals. His imagination was such that even the blind man, at times, believed he could see. The other man would encourage him in these brief illusions:

—*Get rid of your cane, you're on the right path.*

A lie: Estrelinho still couldn't see a palm tree in front of his nose. Nevertheless, the blind man did not accept his sightlessness. He embodied the old adage: he was the legless man who was always trying to kick. Only at night would he become discouraged, suffering from fears older than humanity. He understood that which, in the human race, is the least primitive: the animal.

—*Does it trouble you that there is no light at night?*

—*Trouble is having a white bird spread its wings in your sleep.*

A white bird? In your sleep? The place for birds is in the heights. They even say God made the heavens to justify birds. Estrelinho tried to mask his fear of omens with subterfuge:

—*And now, Little Gigito? Now, looking up in this direction, am I facing the sky?*

What could the other man say? For a blind man, the sky is everywhere. It was with night's arrival and his guide fast asleep that Estrelinho lost his footing. It was as if a new darkness had appeared inside him. Slowly and stealthily he nested his hand in that of his guide. The only way to fall asleep. Is the clam's shyness the reason for its shell? The following morning, the blind man admitted: *If you die, I've got to die right after you. If not, how do I find the way to heaven?*

It was in the month of December that they took Little Gigito away. Took him from the world to send him to war: they required his military services. The blind man protested: the boy could un-come of age. And the service the boy provided him was life-giving and lifelong. The guide called Estrelinho aside and calmed him down:

—*Don't go lonering around now. I already sent for my sis to take my place.*

The blind man stretched his arm as if hoping to hold onto their goodbye. But the other was no longer there. Or had he turned away on purpose? Then, with neither time nor tide, Estrelinho listened as his friend pulled away, engulfed, fargotten, inevitably invisible. For the first time, Estrelinho felt disabled.

—*Now, only now, am I one who turns a blind eye.*

In the minutes that followed, the blind man spoke loudly, all to himself, as if conjuring the presence of his friend: *Listen, my brother, listen to this silence. The mistake people make is to think that all silences are the same. They're not: there are distinct qualities of silence. It's like this. The dark, this snuffed-out nothingness that these eyes of mine touch: each one is unique, colourless in its own way. Understand me, brother Gigito?*

But a response from Gigito never came, and silence followed, this one, yes, repeated and the same. Dis-tended to,

Estrelinho stood watching the in-sights, his eyes surrounded by sunspots and milky no-ways. It was a moonless night, its dark dye unending. Squinting, the blind man took in the darkness, its shapes and its fragments. The world bruised his uncoupled hand. His solitude hurt like a kink in a giraffe's neck. He recalled the words of his guide:

—*Lonely and sad is rheum in a blind man's eye.*

Fearing the night, he set off wandering, staggering along. His theatrical fingers played the role of eyes. Stubborn as a pendulum he went, choosing a route. Stumbling, snagging, he ended up falling down on the side of the road. There he fell asleep, his dreams zigzagging in search of Little Gigito's hand.

Then, for the first time, he saw the heron. Just as Little Gigito had described: the soaring bird, white like dawn. Its wings throbbing, as though its body occupied no space at all.

Anguished, he averted his empty gaze. It was a vision to invite misfortunes. When he returned to himself, it seemed as if he knew the place he'd stumbled upon. As Gigito would say: that was a place that snakes came to refill their venoms. But he couldn't muster the strength to leave.

He remained on the side of the road, like a balled-up handkerchief soaked with sadness, one of those that always appear at separations. Until the timid touch of a hand on his shoulders roused him.

—*I'm Gigito's sister. My name is Infelizmina.*

From then on, the girl led the blind man. She did so with great care and long silences. It was as if Estrelinho had, for a second time, lost his sight. The young girl showed absolutely no talent for invention. She described each snippet of the landscape with reason and factuality. The world the blind man had come to know dimmed. Estrelinho no longer had the lustre of fantasy. He stopped eating, stopped asking, stopped complaining. Weak, he wanted someone to carry him along, no longer just his hand but his entire body. At each turn, she pulled the blind man to her. He went along feeling the roundness of her breasts, his hand no longer sought only another hand. Until, at last, he accepted the invitation of desire.

That night, for the first time, he made love, intoxicated and overcome. In an instant, Gigito's teachings returned to him. What before had been scarce became abundant and the seconds surpassed eternities. His head swooped like a swallow and he let his heart be guided like bats: by the echo of passion. For the first time, the blind man felt sleep come over him without any anguish. And he fell asleep curled up in the girl, his body imitating fingers dissolved in another hand.

In the middle of the night, however, Infelizmina awoke, mugged by alarm. She'd seen the great white heron in her dream. The blind man felt a thud, as if wings had beat against his chest. But he feigned tranquility and began to soothe the girl. Infelizmina returned to bed, night-drowned.

The morning brought the news: Gigito had died. The messenger was brief, as a soldier ought to be. His message resonated infinitely, as the wounds of war ought to. It was strange the way the blind man reacted without the least surprise, as if he were already aware of the loss. The girl stopped speaking, orphaned of her brother. From that death on, she only grew sadder, withering away. And so she remained, unable to resume her life. Until the blind man approached and led her to the house's veranda. Then he began to describe the world, outdoing himself as he detailed the heavens. Little by little, a smile began to spread: the girl's soul was healing. Estrelinho befancied all manner of lands and landscapes. Yes, the girl agreed. She'd slumbered in such landscapes before she was born. She looked at the man and thought: I held him in my arms before this life. And when she had already shaken loose her sadness, she risked the question:

—*All this, Estrelinho? All this exists where exactly?*

And the blind man, confident in stride and course, responded:

—*Come, I'll show you the way!*

The Delivery

———◆———

The couple approached in dual obscurity. Both asked the shadow to pass. The woman was more bent over than a cave on the side of a mountain. She was pregnant, nearly to term. Arriving at the light, they declared themselves to be Diamantinho, the nearest neighbour among the village residents, and his rotund wife, Tudinha Rosa, writhing in pains and grimaces. The poor thing woozier and woozier, swimming in a sea of dizziness. Diamantinho, however, appeared aloof to his wife.

The couple showed up at the home of Ananias and Maria Cascatinha, their affable neighbours. The two ladies stood on the veranda, a mat extending for come-what-may. Maria Cascatinha smiled, timidiminutive: that was her most personal mat. It wasn't a simple object for sitting. On that mat, all her children, amid cooing and moaning, had been conceived.

Diamantinho entered, granting himself perch and position, more homeowner than house guest. He sat, ordered a drink, made use of the comforts. Ananias, the host, even called for his attention: Was he not going to help his bowed wife? The other only smiled, savouring pleasures of this and other lives. Ananias insisted:

—*You, Diamintinho, don't you share in the family suffering?*

—*You're right, Ananias, I only think about from my gut to here. Truly, I'm not worth her troubles. But I've been like this ever since my father's belly.*

Of his wife, Diamantinho made no mention. Tudinha Rosa remained outside on her back, unwound. Nevertheless, she'd declined the mat. Childbirth ought to take place above the earth, mother of mothers. Such is tradition's commandment. Maria Cascatinha gave thanks that the mat was spared. Then she rolled it up carefully in the corner. Tudinha now sat above the world. But the earth's caress hardly relieved her. The woman remained in pain: her eyes uneven, her insides imploding.

In the other room, her husband enjoyed the beverages offered, his eyes wandering lazily. And he continued threading conversation, always in the most concise inexactitude:

—*I feel rusty, Ananias. It's not that I may be older than you. It's that I was born before…*

Ananias was growing irritated with the visitor's attitude, more insistent in his indifference than a pangolin. It's well known: childbirth is a matter for women alone. Diamantinho, meanwhile, seemed far too aloof. And, more seriously, things were growing complicated outside. Tudinha regressed from open-eyed to cross-eyed. She mixed up everything, even prayers: the Hail Father and the Our Mary. Distressed, Ananias proposed actions and precautions. Wouldn't it be better to bring the expectant woman to town? The candidate for father, serene as a river in the flatlands, didn't seem to care. He ordered Ananias to sit still. Then he extended his cup to request another top-up. All without hesitation.

The woman, his irrefutable wife, was doubled over, shrieking and screaming. Several young girls gathered in a circle, all bent forward over the suffering mother. The nervous circle of women could be seen through the window. Finally, Ananias was summoned to help. Ananias suggested the two of them lend assistance, but the other man responded that he was finishing his drink. After that he would leave, at a time and in a mood to fulfill his duty. For now, he peeled back time, impassible like the trunk of a baobab tree.

Ananias broke with tradition, joining the delivery that dragged and the midwives who were growing uneasy. Fundamental doubts grew. Everyone, after all, knows: a drawn-out delivery signals a wife's infidelity. To save the situation, the expectant mother should admit her sin, divulge the name of the child's true father. If she doesn't, then the baby remains stuck in the womb, with neither month nor sign.

Then, amidst cries, sighs, and so much perspiring, Tudinha Rosa confessed to trading affections with Ananias, the very same and present host. Maria Cascatinha entered a state of not-even-there: her husband, father of a strange bud? However, she continued her midwife's toils, unalterable. Only her eyes defied her, spilling over. Without a word, she finished the work of disbellying her sudden adversary. In the beginning, Tudinha's confession had been a simple murmur, going unheard beyond the vicinity. During her final efforts, however, the gestant went on praising the consummated betrayal:

—*It was Ananias, it was him!*

Inside, all was heard. It was as if the world had split open in rocks and rifts. Diamantinho, amid the outburst, turned from sunrise to sunset.

He went out to the veranda looking every bit the husband, with airs of hard looks and hard fists. In a word: shocked and shaken. He moved from fellow to guy, from guy to so-and-so. Never before was such metamorphosis seen. He grew enraged to the point of blades and grenades. He yelled threats and improprieties: he, Ananias, must kiss the feet that trampled him. Between the two men, resounding blows ensued.

As pummels and insults were traded, the new boy migrated toward the light. Diamantinho and Ananias took no notice of the birth. Tudinha and the newborn were brought to an inside room. Ananias, reeling from so many drubbings, retreated into the same room as his respective expectant. There he stayed for many lifetimes. From the living room, Diamantinho gusted with furies, invoking vexes and the evilest eye against

Ananias. Then he wore himself out, miserable as a peel without the banana. Maria Cascatinha, appearing with equal sorrow, came to the aid of the betrayed Diamantinho. She laid her arm on his shoulder and told him she'd accompany him homeward. They say Maria Cascatinha never returned. Not even to fetch the sacred mat.

The Perfume

———◆———

Today we're going dancing! is how Justino announced himself, extending hands full of a package the colour of a gift. Gloria, his wife, wasn't sure how to accept it. He was the one who ended up untying the knots and pulling from the colourful wrapping paper a dress no less vivid. The woman, accustomed to living low, had spent so long waiting she'd already forgotten what it was she was waiting for. Justino oversaw the railroad, one hour fused with the next, one enormous cloud of steam, a minute hand buried in his heart. Time, that stale thief of spontaneity, was an uninvited guest driving a wedge between husband and wife. What remained was a landscape of weariness, uninterest, and uh-huhs. Love—in the end, what was the point?

Which is why Gloria was so startled, leaving the dress dangling across her lap. What was she waiting for, why didn't she get ready? Her husband seemed to have played a joke on her. What had happened to him? He had always guarded her so jealously that she could barely appear at the window, much less anywhere else. Gloria stood up and dragged the dress along with her to the bedroom. Incredulous, she sleepwalked the comb sluggishly through her hair. In vain. Her untidiness had resulted in permanent braids. Gloria remembered her mother's words: an emancipated black woman is one who knows what to do with her own hair. *But, Mother: First off, I'm of mixed race. Secondly, I've never known this thing called freedom.* She laughed at herself: free? It seemed like a word from another language. Just spelling it out caused her embarrassment, the same kind she tasted when putting on the dress her husband had given her. She opened the drawer, winning the battle with the stubborn wood. She grabbed the bottle of perfume, old but still in its packaging. It weighed very little, the liquid had long since evaporated. Justino had given her the perfume when they began seeing each other, she still a girl. It had been the only preesent she had received in her entire life. But now there was the dress. She squeezed the perfume bottle, milking the final drops. *What did I use this perfume on?* she asked herself as she tossed the bottle toward the void beyond the window.

—*I don't even know what wearing perfume feels like.*

She listened to the old bottle shatter on the sidewalk. She turned back toward the living room, her dress going one way, her body the other. The hem of the dress nibbled at her shoes.

She dreaded what her husband would say, he was always pointing out when she went too far. This time, however, he had an unusual look, as though he didn't believe his eyes. He pulled her to him and adjusted her lines, lifting the dress a bit higher, until it was nearly nipping at her waist.

—*You're not going to put a little something on your face then?*

—*A little something on my face?*

—*Yeah, a little colour, a little polish or whatever.*

Gloria didn't know what to think. She turned around and headed for the bathroom, mouth agape. What had come over him, was he ill? Where the devil had that lipstick gone, the one that had spent years on the shelf collecting dust? She found it, hardly more than a stub, worn down by the kids' playing. She applied some to her lips. Lightly, only a shadow of colour. *Load some more on, put the red ones to use.* Her husband was talking to her in the mirror. She lifted her head, a stranger to herself.

—*Yes, we're going to the dance. Did you used to dance, before?*

—*And the children?*

—*I already made arrangements with the neighbour, don't worry about that.*

And off they went. Justino had to push the little truck. As always, she got out to lend a hand. But her husband refused: no, not this time. And he pushed the truck alone, where had anyone ever seen such a thing?

37

They finally arrived. Gloria's expression suggested she couldn't take in the reality. She sat there on the old truck's seat. Justino gently-manned the situation, hand extended, arm at the ready to hold doors. The dance had brought people from all around, full to the stitches. The music flowed throughout a dance hall swarming with couples. They found a table and sat down. Gloria's eyes did not do their work. They merely gazed bashfully at the table.

Then, a man came up to them, his conduct respectful, and asked the brakeman if he'd allow his wife to take a gentle-manly spin around the dance floor. Her eyes, full of terror, waited for the storm to blow in. But it didn't. Justino looked at the young man and gave his consent. Gloria responded:

—*But I'd like to have the first dance with my husband.*

—*You know I never dance…*

As she still hesitated, he ordered her, his command feigning tenderness: *Go, my Gloria, have fun!*

And she went—slowly, still startled. As she twirled around the floor, she never took her eyes off her man, sitting there at the table. She looked deep into his eyes and saw there an abandonment she couldn't quite put her finger on, like the last of her old perfume. That's when she understood: her husband was offering her to the world. The dance, that invitation, they were a farewell. Her chest confirmed this suspicion when she saw her husband stand up and prepare to leave. She cut the dance short and ran to Justino.

—Where are you going, husband?

—A friend called me, he's outside. I'll be right back.

—I'll go with you, Justino.

—Outside is no place for a woman. Stay, dance with the boy. I'll be back soon.

Gloria didn't return to the dance. Sitting at the table he'd reserved for them, she raised her husband's glass to her lips and left her lipstick on it. She stood watching Justino disappear amid the smoke in the dance hall, bearing himself far away. Countless times she'd seen this retreat, her husband rendered faceless amid the steam of train engines. This time, however, she felt something in her chest, the arrhythmia of a hiccup. At the threshold of the doorway, Justino turned his head back for one more long look at his wife. In surprise, he saw an unprecented tear glistening as it ran down her half-hidden face. Tears, after all, are water, and only water can wash away our sorrows. Justino felt something stumble in his chest, ash turning to ember in his heart. And the night came to an end, the door cut through that shortlived commotion. Gloria collected the tear from her cheek with the shoulder of her dress. To whom, within herself, was she saying her goodbyes?

She left the dance and set out into the dark night. She looked for the old truck. She held out hope she would still find it there, in need of a push. But there was no sign of Justino. She walked home to the sound of chirping crickets. Halfway home, she took off her shoes so her feet could feel the sand's warm caress. She gazed at the starlit sky. Stars are the eyes of those who died for love. They look down upon us from above, proof that only love can concede immortality.

She arrived home too exhausted to feel tired. For a second, she thought she saw signs that Justino was there. But her husband, if he had been there, had taken his tracks with him. Gloria lost her appetite to go on living there, their home wounded her like a portrait of the departed. She dozed off on the front steps.

She woke up early the next morning, in a daze between sleep and dream: she felt, inside herself, with only her soul's senses to guide her, the scent of perfume. Where could it be coming from? Could it be coming from her old perfume bottle? No, it could only be from a new present, a gift of the passion she began to feel once again.

—Justino?!

Leaping to her feet, she ran inside the house. That's when she stepped on the tiny bits of glass, scattered beneath her window. To this day, one can find the indelible tracks on the living-room floor from when Gloria shed the first drops of her bloody glee.

Virigílio's Heel

———◆———

Hortência is dressed in her sorrows and her rags. Morning presses on under a hot sun as she trails her husband's casket. She's alone at the funeral, with only a few old ladies. No one cries. It's as if the deceased has left no living relative. Hortência walks through the rain, intransitive amid the transiting public. She always dreads roadways, the way they act like they own the place, laying down laws wherever they go. She doesn't even own her home. But on this present procession, she's already lost all fear, as though her feet and the pavement have traded intimate secrets.

As a matter of fact, during the deceased's lifetime, she walked many times up and down that street. Repeatedly, night after night, she came to the rescue of her late husband Filimone, derailed on his way back from the bar. On mistified nights, she'd pick up her husband on some unknown roadside and help him pair his feet with his footsteps. When it came to Filimone, alcohol brought one advantage: he let loose under its influence, becoming a boy to his wife, the child of her boundless tenderness. In all else, her

41

husband left a record of good-for-nothingness. The place he'd spent the longest: his mother's belly. All those years, he lived at the expense of her kindness, insensitive to her pleas.

—*Me, drunk? Look, Hortência, I can even walk on my feet!*

The drink caused his blood to ferment, making him unfit for fatherhood, demoting him to mere husband. For his wife, Filimone had only abuse.

—*They've taken everything from me, woman. Now the only thing left for me is to do you wrong.*

She grew used to it. For days in a row, Hortência would leave the house in search of her husband. She did the full tour of roadsides and ditches, leaning over to help a sprawled-out Filimone to his feet at each one.

But now she'll never have to carry his weight again. This will be his body's final trip. She's spent all their money on the funeral. A car would be too much of an expense. And so the casket rides atop a *tchovaxitaduma*, a wagon pulled by human hands. The slats of wood don't quite line up, and the light, sliced and refracted, allows a view of the body at rest inside. The casket is made of scrap wood. Hortência gathered tables, chairs, and crates. She cobbled together all that wood to give her husband that dark fate. The neighbourhood carpenter, Virigílio the Nail, charged no labour.

—*It's a labour of the heart. One day I die, the next day it's you*, he said.

Besides, they were drinking buddies, he and the deceased. But his work is beyond imperfect. The carpenter came up with all sorts of excuses:

—In the houses of the dead, we can't do too much work. It brings bad luck.

What's more, the best wood is set aside for adorning life. And he went on making excuses, fearful of that fatal subject. Today it's your day, tomorrow it's ours. And on and on, all drool and spit. His shirt sleeve came to his aid to resolve a runny nose.

—The world is so ugly, so full of bad ends. So much that it's only worth looking at with the help of some beer. Don't you agree with me, Hortêncinha?

Hortêncinha? What is that all about? The man started with the diminutive, this marker of intimacy, and then descended into worse behaviour. Did the carpenter intend to charge for his work after all, by the kiss? Hortência didn't bother to resist, limper than Filimone in his casket. She gave herself up to the woodworker's assault. She was empty, her sorrow had robbed her of any reasonable sense.

—That's just how it is, Hortência: today dies today.

Virigílio and the nail. For Hortência, it didn't really matter whether he hammered or he didn't. Certain animals play dead to survive. She played the animal.

At the funeral, however, Virigílio is nowhere to be found. Hortência could use his help; never has she felt such need of support. Calm down. After all, the carpenter hinted at the likelihood of his absence. Half a word to the wise is all they need to understand.

—Maybe even I won't be able to go. In this cold weather, all my heels seize up.

43

At the cemetery, the widow was unable to cry, so great was her sorrow. Tears are quick to flow from those of us who still harbour hope. The older ladies approached the grave. They shed tears, but without any heart to their crying. Hortência drove the other women away. Said she wanted to go home, put things in order. What things? the women asked each other. And then they left, disappointed they could no longer dine on others' misfortunes.

Who knows, some said, maybe she hasn't embraced widowhood. You can't see so much as a drop of sadness: can that really be? There's been no understanding Hortência since the deceased's passing. They demand that her sorrow be familiar, lending itself to comment by a thousand tongues, capable of being spread wide in chaotic disorder. But Hortência's melancholy, so personal and unique, strikes fear into the women. And so, all the women make themselves strangers.

The only company that remained for her was the carpenter. He always arrived after hours, having lost time's plumbline. And then it became common to see something else that, in that neighbourhood, had never been witnessed before: Hortência, head aswirl with drink, making her way back from the bar. The widow spilled through the dirt streets. What had caused her to give herself over to drink with such fury? Who knew? The truth is a lie that speaks a language different from that of thought. Hortência explained:

—*I'm wandering in search of my Filimone. He must have stumbled somewhere around here.*

44

And so, before Filimone and after Filimone, the woman has never known the taste of sleep, not at night nor for a moment's rest. Is Hortência all eyes and no rest? There are no witnesses who could say. Only the carpenter interrupts the widow's solitary existence. The two of them adding up to a personal and incommunicable state of inebriety. And they laugh, with joys that don't belong to this world. These meanwhiles are brief, and any infatuation nonexistent.

—*If one day I slip, sleepy, into the ditch, would you catch me, Virigílio the Nail?*

—*Without any doubt, Hortência. Today it's my turn, tomorrow's it's yours: that's life…*

Until one night, a chill in the air reminds the widow that it has been exactly one year since Filimone's funeral. At this point, Hortência couldn't even recognize the right side from the wrong side of her sober heart. Her husband's death: did it happen in the verse or inverse of her real life? She closes her eyes and sorrow floods over her. Hortência tries summing up her life. But this isn't something that can be quantified. A single thought dominates her mind: she needs to send off her distant husband a second time.

Hortência dries her tears and decides right then: she will set off into the dark, straight for the cemetery. She hasn't filled her basket with the time-honoured offerings to the dead—capulanas and flour—but with beer bottles by the dozen. She's even stopped by the house of her husband's companion Virigílio the Nail to see

45

if he'll join her solitary procession. Virigílio explains that he will, but she should go on ahead, making an opening in the mist, he'll be along shortly, of course, and so on and so forth:

—*Today it's my turn, tomorrow, it's everyone else's.*

Hortência understands the message: solitude and that soulless path are hers alone. She arrives, sits down next to the grave, and begins cracking open the beers. She drinks and drinks, her lips those of the deceased in the soil.

—*Drink up, Filimone. Now I no longer have to pick you up.*

Later, having traded glances with her husband, Hortência starts back through the dark. Who knows what, whether it's the mist or such human inhumanity, that leads the widow to the bottom of a ditch. Some claim they saw pieces of her clothing spread along the frigid ground. If there were any witnesses, not a single one raises a hand to relieve her suffering. What they do is to alert Virigílio the Nail. It was he who should go there. After all, Hortência is his company. But the carpenter takes a look at the cold, damp fog and and then at his heel, recalling the way sharp little pains always pricked him when the weather shifted:

—*Today, each one of us. Tomorrow, not a soul.*

Down in the cold ditch, Hortência is overcome with a sleepiness greater than the night. *What's happening?* she asks. *How is it I'm lying in the dirt but know no rest?* Then she moves around until she's nestled in the night's womb. Or, who knows, perhaps she's looking for the right position so Filimone's arms can find her.

Rain

———◆———

I've been seated at the window watching the rain fall for three days now. How I've missed the soggy rin-a-tin-tin of each raindrop. The perfuming earth reminiscent of a woman on the eve of affection. How many years has it been since it last rained like this? Having lasted so long, the drought had slowly silenced our suffering. The heavens watched the earth's progressive decline and saw their own death mirrored. We intirrigated ourselves: was it still possible to begin anew, was there still a place for joy?

The rain is falling outside, melodic and divine. The ground, this indigenous indigent, soon blossoms with various beauties. I sit watching the street below as though looking through a window onto the entire country. As the pools of water swell and swell, Tristereza tidies up the room. For Aunt Tristereza, the rain isn't a meteorological matter but a message from the spirits. The old woman adopts a wide smile: this time, for sure, I'll slip on the suit she insists so much that I wear. Such a fine piece of clothing and here I am donning short sleeves and blue jeans.

Tristereza shakes her head back and forth at my stubborness: what justification could I have for such a dishevelled look, for not attending to proper appearances? She doesn't understand.

As she smoothes out the sheets, she moves onto other topics of conversation. The elderly lady harbours no doubts: the rain is an answer to prayers, to ceremonies honouring our ancestors. In all Mozambique, the war is coming to a halt. Now the rain can fall once again. All these years, the gods reproached us with this drought. Deep underground, the dead—even those gone for some time—had begun drying up. Tristereza begins brushing off the coat I'll never use and offers up her certitudes:

—*Our land was full of blood. Today, it's being wiped clean, like these clothes here I'm washing. But not even now, you'll pardon this plea, not even now you'll give this suit of yours its turn?*

—*But Aunt Tristereʒa: couldn't it be all this rain is a bit too much?*

—*Too much? No, the rain hasn't forgotten how to fall*, says the old woman. And she explains: *Water knows how many grains are to be found in the sand. For each grain, the water forms a drop. Just like the mother who knits a sweater for her missing child.* Tristereza believes nature has its own ways of working, unfolding in simple ways just like hers. The rains were conferred on us at the right moment: the displaced who return to their homes will arrive to find the ground damp, just as the seedlings prefer it. Peace acts according to its own laws, free from the will of politicians.

Yet inside me, a certain distrust persists: will this rain, my dear lady, not prove too long and too much? Is the calamitous drought not being followed by a punishing rain?

Tristereza looks around at the drenched landscape and shows me other meteorological insights that my wisdom cannot reach. You can always recognize a printed cloth by its reverse side, she's fond of telling me. God made us white and black so that, on the backs of one and the other, He might decipher mankind. And pointing to the hefty clouds, she declares:

—*Up there, sir, there are fish and crabs. That's right, animals that always follow the water.*

And she adds: Without fail, these critters rain down during a storm.

—*You don't believe me, sir? They've even fallen right inside my house.*

—*OK*, I say, pretending I believe her. *What kinds of fish?*

Negative: such fish can't be named. To do so, sacred words would be necessary and such words aren't fit for our human voices. And again she casts her gaze toward the window. Outside, the rain continues. The heavens are giving back the sea it had sheltered with lazy azure migrations. But it looks as if the heavens intend, in so doing, to overrun the entire earth, joining its rivers, shoulder to shoulder. I come back to my question: Won't the waters prove too much, falling with such malignant generosity? Tristereza's voice repeats itself in a diluvial monotone. She murmurmuses: *You, sir, you'll forgive my tongue, look like a creature in search of the forest.* And she adds:

—*The rain is washing the sand clean. The dead will be pleased. It would be a show of respect your using this suit. To match this celebration of Mozambique...*

Tristereza holds her gaze on me, in doubt. Then, resigned, she hangs up the jacket, which seems to let out a sigh. My stubbornness dangles on a hanger. I glance toward the street; streaks of sorrow drip down the windows. What is it I'm always trying to escape? What reasons does the old woman have for accepting her confinement, all dressed for home? Perhaps for belonging more to the world, Tristereza doesn't feel, as I do, the lure to leave. She thinks the time of suffering has passed, that our land is being washed of its past. I have my doubts. I need to observe the street. Windows: are they not the place where houses dream of being the outside world?

The old woman finishes her work, says goodbye as she closes the doors, lingering and languid. Sorrow has crept into her soul and I'm its cause. I notice the plants outside sprouting from the earth. The colour green speaks the language of all the others. The old lady has already begun to repeat her goodbyes and is leaving when I call to her: .

—*Tristereza, grab my suit.*

She suddenly gleams with surprise. As she undresses the hanger, the rain begins to stop. Only a few remaining drops of water fall on my coat. Tristereza urges me: *Don't brush them off, these little drops are good luck.* And arm in arm, we both step out into the pools of water, carefree as children who see in the world the joy of a neverending game.

Felizbento's Pipe

Every tale loves to masquerade as the truth. But words are nothing more than smoke, too weightless to stick to the present reality. Every truth aspires to be a tale. Facts dream of becoming words, sweet fragrances running from the world. You'll see in this case that it's only in the fiction of our wonderment that the truth meets the tale. What I'm about to report here took place in a peaceful land, one where Sundays outnumber the days of the week.

That land was still just beginning, newly born. The seeds there found a welcoming home, and green spread across the lush landscapes. Life was linked to time, the trees scaling great heights. One day, however, war landed, with its capacity for all manner of death. From then on, everything changed and life became much too mortal.

The nation sent workers in a rush. The representatives in the capital always act quickly when they're far from home.

They told the living they must leave, converting them from home-towners to homeless. Security reasons. They called the residents one by one, in unalphabetical order. It was Felizbento's turn. The old man listened, as incredulous as a frog that gobbles a snake. He consisted of nothing more than a sigh. He carried on as he had before, winding his soul. The others were condensed, packed up and bundled, on the backs of trucks. But Felizbento stood firm. An official took charge of the situation, ordering him to get to it. To leave, just like the others.

—Didn't you hear the order? Now get to it.

Felizbento applied a second coat of silence, rubbed one foot against the other, shining his shoeless feet. Or was he pointing at the earth, the only place he'd ever lived? He'd always silenced his suffering, armed with patience greater than his age. Finally, he pointed to the sprawling forest and said:

—If I'm to leave here, I need to take all these trees with me.

The nation's servant ran out of patience and told Felizbento that, a week later, they'd return to take him away, even if they needed to use brute force. And then they left.

The next day the man set to unearthing the trees, digging them up by the roots. He began with the sacred tree in his backyard. He dug in deep: there in the place he'd been hollowing out, total darkness had been set free. To continue his burrowing, he grabbed a Petromax lamp, the kind he'd got in Johannesburg. And day after day, he spent long hours at work.

His wife, disappointed, pointed out the unsuitability of his actions. It wasn't worth asking anything of Felizbento. The clothes of the dead no longer wrinkle. The obstinance of old age doesn't bend. The wife remained perched in the window like a stopped clock. In the black of night, the old woman saw only the movement of the Petromax, which looked as if no hand guided it.

Her heart heavy, the woman sketched out a plan. She would offer herself, as in the times when their bodies believed they had no limits. She reached deep into one of the closets, where not even cockroaches dared to tread. She snatched the floral-stamp dress, some high heels. And she began her nocturnal wait, clothes and perfumes tantalizing. She remembered an old saying of Felizbento's, from times past:

—If you wish to make love, nighttime is the best.

Those who've loved time and again know the heat of the night, this bed of beds. At night, creatures change in value. The day reveals the world's defects: wrinkles, dust, lines—in the light, everything can be seen. At night, though we look more intensely, we see less. Each creature reveals itself only by the light it gives off. On this particular night, she emitted a soothing glow like that of the moon.

Felizbento arrived home from his toils, glanced at his wife. He was like a beached whale, the water that'd carried him there suddenly gone. His wife drew closer, touching his arm. She looked every bit her own woman, this was her irrefusable beauty.

—Stay with me tonight. Forget the trees, Felizbento.

Dizzied, the old man still hesitated. The woman wrapped her body in his, her fingers creeping across his skin. Felizbento felt like water in a fish. What could that be? Did that soul belong to this world? That's when, incidentally, she stepped on her husband's bare foot with her high heels. Her shoe was like a needle on a balloon. The farmer recoiled, determined. Machete back in hand, he went out to meet the blackness once again.

Then one day, Felizbento came back up to the surface and asked his wife to unpack his suit, get the proper clothes in order, to starch the fabrics. It had been more than thirty years since those clothes had been put to their use. His shoes no longer even fit. His feet had grown misshapen with barefootedness. In fact, there wasn't a shoe to be found that fit him.

He took the old shoes with him all the same, half-covering his feet, treading on his heels. He dragged them across the floor, lest his feet be separated from his footsteps. And off he went, as bent as a reed, in this youthfulness that's only to be found in old age. He began to enter the land and, only once, he turned back. Not to say farewell, but to rummage through his pockets for something forgotten. His pipe! He went through his clothes. He took out his old pipe and spun it in his fingers, beneath the trembling light of the burning lamp. Then, in a gesture of dejection, he threw it away. As if discarding his entire life.

There the pipe remained, remote and forgotten, half buried in the sand. It looked as if the earth gave it breath, smoking the useless utensil. Felizbento descended into the hole, disappearing.

To this day, his wife crouches over the hole and calls after him. Not yelling, but calling sweetly, as if to someone in his sleep. She still wears the floral dress, high heels, and perfume with which, in the midst of her despair, she attempted to seduce him. After a while, she draws back, snuffed out. Only her eyes, roundly insistent, resemble an insomnious owl. What dreams called that woman into existence?

Those who've returned to that place say that, beneath the sacred tree, there now grows a plant fervent with green, climbing an invisible arbour. And they give assurances that this little tree grew from nothing, sprouting from some old, forgotten pipe. And, at the sunset hour, when the shadows no longer try so hard, the tiny tree puffs out smoke just like a chimney. As far as his wife is concerned, there is no doubt: beneath Mozambique, Felizbento is smoking his old pipe in peace. As he waits for a capitalized and definitive Peace.

The Flag in the Sunset

Daybreak. The sun marking five o'clock. The shadows, blurry billows, begin to rise amid the drowsiness that blankets the morning. On the treetops, birds bloom. Each morning provides confirmation: nothing, in this world, comes about all of a sudden. The light began climbing in the sky some time earlier, like a bright caterpillar gnawing away at the husk of darkness. Creatures appear one by one beneath the depths of inexistence. At this embryonic instant, the world is in transition. The sky becomes a deeper blue, permeavisible. April: Yes, of course it must be April. Now that the sunrise has become part of this story, let's get straight to the point.

On a recent morning, a child came sauntering up the road. Who was this boy who made the world boyish? We'll leave out his name, we'll forget the place he came from. In addition to the boy, only his grandmother stood out: the boy was intimate with the world beyond. Now and then, the child handed her the knife and made his request.

—*Cut me, Grandma!*

To dream, the boy needed to bleed. His grandmother ceded to his demands, as accustomed to this blade as some mothers are a comb. The blood came forth and the world saw its future, as though its ear were put to time's expectant belly. Such were the sayings of the old woman—but who paid her any attention?

What's certain is that the boy continued his course that morning. His feet chose his path among the stones, they had no need for eyes to find their way. The boy walked past the municipal building, the only one in the village. He turned his head to look at the flag. The banners danced in the sky, a wrinkle of light. An old coconut tree missing its canopy served as a mast. So ragged were the flag's colours that not a single part of it rainbowed. The child's eyes fireflied against the light: that was when he felt the blow that dropped him to the ground. An extracranial explosion in his head. The voice of an authoritarian soldier descended:

—*Didn't you see the flag?*

Spread across the road, across the stones his feet had been evading, the boy took in the surroundings overhead. A coconut tree aroused a coastal reminiscence. Wherever a palm tree is to be found, there ought to be a sea, an endless line of receding waves. The boy, cast down on the sudden dirt, wondered at so much open sky. Which leads him to the muddy question: why is the ground so firm beneath him? Another blow, the soldier's heavy boot sends his face to meet the earth. The boy lay there, unable to see beyond the red sand. His thoughts were a jumble. Palm tree, palm near the sea, where the celestial blue plants its roots. He wondered, showing the proper respect: and if men hoisted up not the flag but the earth?

The world continued spinning. The voice hit him once again, like a whip:

—*You, kid. Didn't you learn proper respect for the flag?*

He felt his blood running, the soldier's boot hurting him one last time. How was he to have known the conduct required by the guard? But the soldier was military to the bone: he was only acting out others' ignorance, a lead-wielding judge unable to distinguish between someone who was outside the law and someone who followed laws from outside. The boy began to see another path, so free of stones there was no need for his feet to watch their step. A path that had no need for flags. As the soldier dealt out more brutality, the flag seemed to lose its colours, the landscape grew colder, the light falling to its knees. Well, then.

Then something never seen before or since happened: the flag, with an unexpected lurch, lifted off, a bird in flight nakedly crossing the clouds. Tributary, the banner departed for other skies. At that moment, it became clear how much flags detract from celestial blues.

But the shock was just beginning: this was merely a fore-shadowing. A second later the palm tree hurled itself from the heights, striking the soldier, a ray of light splitting the world in two. The dust rose in chaotic clouds, but soon the palm could be seen once again, unexpectedly lying next to the two bodies.

Some said that the tree was already dead. Few believed it. Most sided with the grandmother's version of the story: the trunk had come undone, liquified, because of the child's death. Revenge for the injustices committed against a life. The only things to be believed were those two deaths, one against the other. The palm had passed on but its absence would be felt forever. Whoever passes that way today still hears the whisper of its leaves. The tree that is no longer there consoles the shadow of a child, a shadow that endures beneath the sun at all hours of the day.

Ninety-Three

———◆———

They came in one by one. The old man headed up the group, his head nodding. As they entered, someone read their names aloud, describing their outfits. Grandchildren filled the room, the great-grandchildren spilled out into the yard. Their grandfather raised his gaze, silent and dim. He smiled the whole time: he didn't want to commit any impoliteness. The old man pretended every birthday. There was no other day throughout the year when they remembered him. They left him there gathering dust with the rest of the objects in the living room.

That night, the gifts piled up and he ran his fingers over each package. His gesture never failed him. After all, there was no hand surer than that of a blind man. The blind man grabbed onto what was there and the rest simply didn't exist. The place where the sightless settled was always the correct one: after all, only those with a choice could err. The old man thanked everyone, a visionless visionary. Everything far from sight, close to heart.

The guests spent a bit of time with him, had no idea what to say, had almost nothing to say, the old man only heard utterances that were louder than a yell. Later, who knew how to measure a blind man? Seeing him in that splendolorous state, they chose to believe—to appease themselves—that their grandfather had fallen asleep. For him, day was just like night, the blind man had to sleep by closing his ears.

But the old man only pretended to be sleeping. In the meantime, he waited for an opening to be able to exercise the most secret of his rogueries. Each day, he escaped from home. When the city began to curb its pulse, he headed for the street. They never noticed his absences. They never imagined that, taking tiny, stumbling footsteps so that he never fell, he sneaked out for a trip to the public park. He went there to meet his two current friends: a feral cat and Ditinho, the street kid, one of those who'd lost his home. The boy carried on a conversation with the old man and in return he offered the kid some small thing stolen from the house. For both of them, the world was enormous. Tired of prodding stories out of the old man, the youngster fell asleep. Softened by the presence of his friend, the old man also applied himself to his park bench, until the cat showed up, more affectionate than the sleep in his eyes. The feline rubbed up against him, his entire body a tongue licking the old man. The animal let forth a sound between purring and wheezing, a rustling in his throat. Were all affectionate cats asthmatic?

Now, sitting among the various noises that resound throughout the house, the old man misses the park. Would it be all right if he stepped out?

—*Step out?*

The entire family was astonished, taken aback. Right then, on the exact day of his birth? Step out where? The old man was resigned; he had given up. They already knew his quirks. For example: three years earlier, he'd decided to construct his own casket. The family wondered: what had happened to him? His oldest daughter shuddered: could it be premonition? Her brothers, on the contrary, laughed: nonsense!

The old man, meanwhile, continued with the casket. A touch one day, a retouch the next. This was our most permanent address, a work for our eternity, didn't it make sense to get it right? You all spend your entire lives working to construct a temporary home; I work toward the definitive one.

For that reason, the family wasn't worried about the old man's wishes. In the middle of the celebration of all his years he wanted to take a long walk alone? A boyish desire, an infantile delirium. And so they left the old man in his arm chair, looking as if he were sleeping. They assured one another that he didn't need looking after. But the illusion of being right is born when everyone is wrong at the very same time. Well, the old man, at that very same moment, proclaimed the following questions:

—*You'll have to excuse me: but, at the end of the day, how old am I now?*

They laughed. The old man was fooling around, he must be pretending to forget. One voice spoke up, informing him of his age. The old man furrowed his brow, suspicious:

—*Ninety-three?*

He seemed thunderstruck. The rest of the night, he rocked his chair in sudden attacks of fright and repeated:

—*Ninety-three?*

Later, the dancers were paired up. The old man, stumbling amidst the couples, walked up to someone: *Excuse me, son, what year is it?*

—*Ninety-three, Dad.*

No, the old man corrected him. *I asked what year it is.* But there was no one there any longer. The noisy multitude increased the rhythm of the festivities. There was no room for grandparents in all that joy. The drinks flowed, and minds slowly turned liquid.

Finally, they brought the birthday cake. The old man blew everywhere except on the cake. They all decided together to snuff out the candles themselves. They cut the cake quickly, they needed to get back to their celebration. The old man must be sleeping over in the corner, they said, he nodded off at any hour of the day. But the old man wasn't sleeping. He was silently lamenting the absence of his street pals, Ditinho and the cat. These two, yes, they were worth his attention. He only felt like a grandfather to them, these vagrants in the park.

Without anyone noticing, the birthday boy ran away from his own birthday. He strolled into the little park and lay down on the bench, breathing with easy happiness. The cat came across the grass and curled up gently against his arm. The old man had kept a treat for him, stolen from the party. Ditinho arrived a short time later, having just dined on trash.

Standing before the bench, the youngster took a curious peek. The old man had never shown up so late. The kid sat down like a member of the family. He placed his hand in the old man's pocket, judged the weight of his wallet, and asked:

—*So then, how much do we have here?*

The old man smiled, raised his hand to his chest, and proclaimed:

—*Ninety-three!*

The boy's eyes lighted up:

—*All that? You're rich, gramps!*

The old man agreed, lighted a smile. The boy's heart was in labour:

—*With all this money, today we're gonna do a bunch of everything: eat, drink, and laugh till we cry.*

And he jumped to his feet, pulling the old man toward a dark little street. The old man suddenly remembered: my cane! But Ditinho answered: from here on out, I'm your cane. And the two walked away, farther and farther from the noisy birthday party. In the park, the cat nostalgically rubbed against the forgotten cane. Then, it slithered through the dark alley, joining its two friends who, already far away, celebrated time, commemorating the day on which all men grow a year older.

Jorojão's Cradle of Memories

My friend Jorge Pontivírgula, Jorojão to us, was telling me about the misunderstandings that plagued his life. Misfortunes that, to hear him tell it, had always come with a dose of presentiment. My friend revealed himself to be what he was: a pre-sentimentalist. But I'll get to that. First, however, I'll give a proper portrait of this Jorge's entire soul.

To sum up his life, Jorojão always had but a single desire: to stay out of trouble. But not even all his fears could stack up to him. His stature exceeded that of a giant. You would look to the clouds as you spoke to him. We used to joke: the man could only kiss sitting down! This Jorojão, in colonial times, circulated through politics like money in a beggar's pockets: changing place often and never finding a home. The din of the city made him ill. To escape to the bush, he offered his services as a safari driver. It's how he used to put distance between himself and the world's bad breath. But that wasn't enough, in the end. For one day he had to drive a delegation of the heads of the PIDE secret police into the forest to hunt. Savage men on a savage hunt: what could be worse? At the end of the day, one of the authoritarian policemen ordered him to clean their guns. Jorojão remembers beginning to tremble:

—*Guns?*

He didn't dare speak the word *guns*, much less touch them. But he acted as if it was no bother at all, and scrubbed, cleaned, and oiled the weapons. As he was doing the last bit of shining, a bullet burst forth at full speed from one of the aforementioned unmentionables. One of the PIDE fell hard as a coconut on a blustery afternoon.

Thirty years having passed, Jorojão excuses himself: *It was just a little bullet, it was nothing at all. The fella really hit the dirt then and there! Aaah, but I can't believe he died from the shot. I think the fright must have given him a heart attack. Or maybe his head wasn't screwed on right.*

He fills his cup again, downs the entire drink in a single gulp. Then, closing his eyes, he clicks his tongue, sharpens his joy anew. Sadness already beginning to creep in, rising to the surface of memory, he feels the need to soak his soul in beer. Rocking his chair back and forth, he explains: it's this seesawing of his chair that transports him to bygone days. If not for the chair he would have already said farewell to all those memories.

The chair must have been rocking quite a bit, because he was retreating once again into the past: after the shot was fired, he was imprisoned for ties to terrorism. A good bit of luck, as it turned out: it was already January of 1974. It didn't take long before the Fascist regime tumbled in April. That morning remains especially unforgettable for him. The masses stormed the prison, went straight to his cell, and carried him in their arms. It was only then that he took measure of his own stature: a giddiness overtook him. He was a hero, a defender of the people.

—*Imagine me there, eh, a guy who never gets involved in anything… If I were to receive an award it would be for keeping out of stuff.*

But the Revolution brought him distinction: he went on to lead one of the newly nationalized companies. Jorojão did his best to refuse. His refusal, however, led to an even bigger mess. So from that moment he performed his functions at the highest level of functionality. Jorojão arrived in the morning and didn't leave until late at night. Everything operated just so, the company coffers filling with profits. Everything was going so well that they began to get suspicious. Other state companies hadn't so much as a plate yet he filled up on soup? An inspection crew showed up, not even bothering to look at his papers. All they needed was to see the gun on the office wall.

—*This gun isn't in line with regulations.*

—*But this is the Glorious Gun, it's the one I used to kill that PIDE bastard, don't you remember, the one whose gun here I was given in a public ceremony?*

His explanation proved to be futile. How could they know if it was the same gun? Mounted on a wall, all guns look the same. They jailed him, charging him with stashing a suspicious shotgun. There he remained, making less noise than a pangolin. He still remembers these unhappy, inglorious times, of falling asleep to forget his belly. The memories still make him bitter.

—*Do you see now, sir? I don't do anything, it's these meddlesome troubles that always come looking for me.*

He stayed in prison for months. One day, through his cell bars, he saw a group of workers from his company enter the prison. He asked to speak to the warden, trying to understand the presence of his subordinates. The prison boss spoke to him with unusual deference:

—*Mr. Jorojão, did you not know that you were to be freed today?*

—*Freed?*

—*Yes, today, in commemoration of World Meteorological Day. However, now you're going to remain here a while longer…*

Why had this been said and undone? The postponement of his release resulted from the following: the workers, longing for their imprisoned director, had performed a witchcraft ceremony to achieve his freedom. The authorities had interrupted the ceremony and arrested the participants, accusing them of arcane superstitions. The cause was now subject to the effect: Jorojão's release would have to be suspended lest the credit for it be given to the feudalist ceremonies. *It's simple*, the head of the prison explained. *If you were to leave now they'd say that these superstitious rites produced their intended effect. And this goes against the principles of materialism. For this very reason, the district also postponed the celebrations for World Meteorological Day.*

Jorojão returned to his cell.

—*Have you ever heard such a thing? They kept me waiting there in prison on account of meteorological materialism!*

Months later he stepped into the freedom of the streets, at a time when no one could any longer tie his release to any stealth-sly spirits. Bitten by the dog and left toothless by the thug, Jorojão lamented. To this day, you can't talk to him about the weather. Sitting in his old rocking chair, the immensity of each day weighs down on him. Work? For what? Work is like a river: even when it's reaching an end, what comes behind it is more and more river. Wearily stretching his legs, he asks me:

—*Who is it who's rocking: me, the chair, or the world?*

Lamentations of a Coconut Tree

The event was official and verified, it made the Nation's newspaper. The buzz about the coconut groves of Inhambane was worthy of headlines and much spilt ink. It all began when, seated along Inhambane's seaside drive, my friend Suleimane Inbraímo split the shell of a coconut. For the fruit didn't gush the usual sweet water, but blood. Exactly so: blood, certified and unmistakable blood. But that wasn't the only astonishing thing. The fruit cried and lamented in a human voice. Suleimane took no exaggerated measures: his wide-open hands dropped the coconut, and the red stains spread. He stood there, dumbfounded and overwhelmed, spent. The shock made his soul vanish into the low tide.

When I ran to help, he was still in the same position, head bent on his chest. Evidence of the incident had been removed, hands washed, amnesiac. Only his voice still trembled as he related the episode to me. I distrusted. Doubt, we know, is the envy that the unbelievable hasn't happened to us.

—*Forgive me, Suleimane: a coconut that spoke, cried, and bled?*

—*I knew it: you weren't going to believe me.*

—*It's not not believing, brother. It's doubting.*

—*Go ahead and ask, among these folk around here, ask about what happened with these coconuts.*

I filled my chest to let my patience breathe. I'm used to strange things. I even have a talent for stumbling on these inoccurrences. But this was not the right moment. We should have left that place long before. Our work had already ended a week earlier and we still awaited news of the boat that would take us back to Maputo. Not that the place wouldn't allow us some modest rest. Inhambane is a city of Arab manners, unpressed to enter time. The tiny houses, dark and light, sighed in the weariness of this eternal measuring of strength between the lime and the light. The narrow streets are good for courting; it appears that in them, no matter how much we walk, we never stray from home.

I watched the bay's feminine blue, this sea that makes no waves nor creates urgency. But my travel companion already had a flea in his ear. When I asked about the arrival of the next boat, Suleimane wobbled, one foot then the other, as prisoners do.

—*Every time, it's coming today.*

The man spoke in imperfect certainty. Because at that very instant, as if issuing from his words, breezes began to swell. It squalled. First, the banana trees fanned. Gesticulant, the leaves swayed listlessly. We didn't make the connection.

After all, only a hint of wind is needed to fan the fruitful plants. They should be called, in that case, fanana trees. But afterward, other greens began to shake in agitated dance. Suleimane began with a stammer:

—*This squall isn't going to abide any boat.*

I sat there, listless a thousand times over, to show I didn't have an opinion. I unwrapped the little cakes I'd bought a short time ago from the ladies at the market. A kid approached. I thought: here comes one more cry-beggar. But no, the child stayed beyond a beggable distance. My teeth had already prepared for the taste when the kid's eyes grew wide, a shout rising in his throat.

—*Mister, don't eat that cake!*

I stopped mid-bite, my mouth in dread of who-knows-what. The boy renewed his sentence: I was not to stick my saliva on the flat cake. He didn't know how to explain, but his mother came at the child's gesticulation. The woman entered the scene with colossal heft, fastening a nimble capulana.

—*The child is right, I'm sorry. These cakes were made with green coconut, were cooked with* lenho.

Only then did I understand: they had offended the local tradition that held the still-green coconut sacred. Forbidden to harvest, forbidden to sell. The unripe fruit, *lenho* as it was called, was to be left amid the tranquil heights of the coconut trees. But now, with the war, outsiders had arrived, placing more faith in money than in the respect for commandments.

—*There are many-many displaced people selling* lenho. *One of these days they'll even sell us.*

But the sacred has its methods, legends know how to defend themselves. Varied and terrible curses weigh over he who harvests or sells the forbidden fruit. Those who buy it get what's left over. The shell bleeding, voices crying, all this was *xicuembos*, hexes with which the forefathers punish the living.

—*You don't believe it?*

The huge woman interrogated me. It wouldn't be long before she reeled off her own versions, applying the principle that two weeks of explanation aren't enough for he who half understood. Even before she spoke, those present clicked their tongues in approval of what she was going to say. In the good country way, each seconds the other. Exclamations of those who, saying nothing, agreed with the unsaid. Only then did the woman unwrap her words:

—*I'll tell you: my daughter bought a basket way over on the edge of town. She brought the basket on her head all the way here. When she tried to take the basket off, she couldn't. The thing looked like it was nailed down. We pulled with all our strength but it didn't budge. There was only one remedy: the girl returned to the market and gave the coconuts back to the man who sold*

them. You hear me? Lend me a bit more of your ear, for a moment.
Don't tell me you didn't hear the story of neighbour Jacinta? No?
And I add, sir: this Jacinta put herself to grating the coconut and
began to see the pulp never had an end. Instead of one pan, she
filled do\zens until fear bid her stop. She laid all that coconut on
the ground and called the chickens to eat it. Then something hap-
pened I almost can't describe: the little chicks were transformed
into plants, wings into leaves, feet into trunks, beaks into flowers.
All, successively, one by one.

I received her reports quieter than a seashell. I didn't want a
misunderstanding. Suleimane himself drank with anguish these
stories of the common man, fanatical believerist. And then
we were gone, leaving that place for a no-star hotel. We had
the common intention to chase sleep. After all, the boat would
arrive the following day. Our return trip was paid for, we no
longer had to think about the spirits of the coconut groves.

Bags and suitcases tottering on deck, motors humming:
that's how, at long last, we made our way back to Maputo.
My animated elbow brushes Suleimane's arm. Only then do
I notice that, hidden amidst his clothes, he carries with him
the cursed coconut. The same one he'd begun to split open.
I marvel:

—*What's this fruit for?*

—*I'm going to send it for analysis at the Hospital.*

Before I could dissent from this logic, he countered: *That*
blood there, who knows in what veins it ran? Who knows if it was

diseased, or rather, disAIDSed? He rewrapped the fruit with an affection meant only for a son. Then he broke off, rocking it with a lullaby. Perhaps it was just this lullaby of Suleimane's, I could almost swear it, and yet he seemed to hear a lament coming from the coconut, a crying from the earth, in the anguish of womanhood.

Beyond the River Bend

What I cite are facts from the newspaper. They went something like this: "A hippopotamus broke into the Centre for Typing and Sewing in the Munhava neighbourhood, leaving a path of destruction and sowing fear among residents of the most densely populated neighbourhood in the capital of Sofala province. [...] A night watchman present at the time said the animal wasn't your regular old hippopotamus, but a very strange specimen who busted down the door to the school, strode into the classrooms, and began to destroy the furniture. [...] Rumours have been circulating among residents in the area that the hippopatomus is in fact a former resident of the city who lost his life in the neighbourhood where the animal came from and that this old man had returned to proclaim the following prophesies: rain would cease to fall in the city and plagues were to kill people by the score. The prediction coincides with a surge in the number of epidemics in the metropolitan region." (End of citation.)

The newspaper didn't cover the remaining events, those that occurred later. What I'm adding to the story here are the reports of those witnesses with faulty judgment, people versed in nocturnal apparitions. Luckily, in our world today, there are no sources undeserving of our trust.

Jordão—or Just J, as he was known—awoke that day in a fit of fear: what were those sounds coming from the school? He froze, abstrained. He decided to sit still and face the consequences of doing nothing. But the racket grew louder. Someone had entered the school in a rage, looking for trouble. Thieves, they must have been. But was it really possible, this level of shamelessness? Was someone testing his courage? Jordão grabbed his gun and headed for the school. He rolled back on his heels, his feet in the opposite gear. The noise coming from the intruder was enough to set the daring running and make a coward of any hero. Fear is a river one must cross wet.

As Jordão drew closer, he called to the heavens for reinforcements: *May the xicuembos protect me!* The moon lit the way. Its glow was strong, but not enough to pull a thorn from your foot. That's the reason Jordão can't be entirely sure of everything he saw, his eyes took in the events that followed but his thoughts found them difficult to grasp. When he looked through the window, he saw the enormous beast chewing through a sewing machine. The mammal's girth was unrivalled by anything he'd ever seen before. This wasn't some ordinary example of his species, this one. A more appropriate name for this beast was hyper-potamus. Just then, the giant beast saw the soldier peeping through the windowframe. He looked straight at the man with the two sleepy eyes stuck to the roof of his forehead. Then, he went back to nibbling on the furniture—the pudgy creature's picnic would not be stopped.

All sorts of ideas began to fly as swift as a flock of birds through Just J's head. How had the *mpfuvo*, as they called the beast in southern Mozambique, come to the school? Had he come in search of knowledge, to learn how to write, out of some thirst to transform from artiodactyl to artiodactypographer? Or had he come to improve his sewing abilities? No, that couldn't be. His fingers were stiffer than panhandles.

During those moments of hesitation, the soldier cast his thoughts back to the way things used to be: those who hunted the *mpfuvo*, in accordance with tradition, never set off for the river without first receiving the blessing of the mystic vapours. Husband and wife would bathe in the medicinal fumes for good luck. When the hunter stuck his prey with the first spear, a messenger would run to the village to alert his wife. From that moment forward, the woman was prohibited from leaving the house. She would light a fire and stand guard over it, without food or drink. Were she to break the ritual, her husband would suffer the wrath of the angry hippopotamus— the hunted turned hunter. Remaining cloistered bounded the beast's spirit, prevented the pachyderm from fleeing the spot where he would meet his end. The wife's confinement would end only when she heard shouts of joy coming from the river, heralding the hunt's success. In the village, everyone except for Just J would rejoice. It always seemed the spears had wounded his soul on that stretch of river.

But now, in the schoolhouse window, it's not jubilant refrains, but the hippopotamus's rage, that makes the soldier stir. In truth, what's provoked the beast's ire at the present moment is the scenery. Corners, doors, walls: this was uncharted territory for the brute. He snarled, gnashed his teeth. The soldier is made tiny by his fear, only his gun grants him any stature. Suddenly, without thinking, Jordão fires a shot. A flurry of bullets hit their mark. The nose, being in front of the eyes, never obstructs them. The beast, in all his girth, trembled and folded, collapsing to the ground. His pink belly lent him the appearance of a newborn. In his final moment he devoted a look full of tenderness to the hunter. As though, instead of resentment, he felt gratitude. Was it love at last sight?

Jordão recalled how, as a child, he'd developed a soft spot for the *mpfuvos* and their clumsy ways: such a large nape for so little neck! Fat as could be, they seemed to him suited to all sorts of dancing. And because the disaster-prone beasts, barely terrestrial, were his brothers: none of them was ever at home among others. Jordão often dreamed about the animals, which looked like upturned canoes riding the river's lazy current. In his dreams, he'd climb on their backs and ride just beyond the river bend. That was his greatest dream: discovering what lay up ahead of the human landscape and reaching the land beyond limits.

At that moment, however, gun in hand, Jordão hungered to lead other lives, to trample other creatures that he found inferior. He was flooded by an abrupt anger for feeling a certain kinship with such untamed creatures. Did this sense of superiority come from his rifle, or had age killed his capacity for imagination? Or do all adults commit this sort of adultery?

The sound of gunshots brought many curious onlookers. They launched straight into he-said, she-said, rage and outrage.

—*You killed the* mpfuvo*? Don't you know who this animal was?*

—*Just wait and see the punishment we'll get on your account.*

—*You won't need to wait until tomorrow. You're going to regret this finger of yours pulled the trigger.*

And off they went. Jordão sat on the top step of the school entrance with his thoughts. All that thinking had made him thinner. What could be done? He'd been accused of killing not some terrible beast but a man transfigured. How could he have guessed at the truth about the hippopotamus, his message-bearing role? He dropped his head into his arms and that's how he remained, more circumflex than the accent mark itself.

That's when he felt a nudge. Someone was tapping him on the back, as though to rouse him from sleep. He looked behind him and goosebumps rose across his entire body. It was a tiny *mpfuvo*, a baby hippopotamus. What could it want, this kid? Shelter is what it sought, the protection of a being greater than itself. He rolled around near the soldier's armpit as if seeking to stir an imaginary breast. Then, he nestled up against his mother's giant body, grunting to call her attention. Jordão regarded the little animal with its mouth bigger than its snout. He rose to his feet and took the orphan into his arms. The little one wouldn't sit still, only making him heavier. Jordão stumbled, nearly dropping his cargo, before regaining his stuttering footsteps along the muddy riverbank.

When they reached the river, the young hippopotamus leaped up to join his herd. As he watched, Jordão felt the weight of his gun grow unbearable. His shoulder began to ache from the load. With an abrupt gesture, he threw the rifle into the river, as though casting off a part of himself. At that moment, he heard a human voice. Where was it coming from? It came from the young hippo he'd just saved.

—*Climb atop the capsized canoe.*

Canoe? That hefty thing cresting the surface? The voice repeated the invitation.

—*Come, I'll show you the place just beyond the river bend.*

Enthralled and disarmed, Jordão climbed atop the dewy dorsal of dreams and set off against the current to the land beyond limits.

Serpent's Embrace

The news on the radio spoke of the unexplained death of Acubar Aboobacar, found in a state of total demise in the vast chair in his living room. And so it went: *by the looks of the direly departed, it's suspected the cause of death was a snakebite. However, neither the animal nor evidence of its bite were found on the deceased's body. The victim's wife told the radio that Aboobacar had of late exhibited strange behaviour and threatened her frequently. Without foundation, he suspected conjugal infidelity.*

What follows is a composite version of the facts and characters, irrepeatably never the same, like the river in which no man ever steps even once.

Mintoninho left the house in a hurry, running through endless green, overgrown fields of grass. He was going to fetch his father, Acubar Aboobacar. The boy didn't want his mother, a merchant at the bazaar, to find her husband missing when she returned home. The kid had grown tired of the household fights that were complicated anew each time his father went on a bender.

On that afternoon, Mintoninho, nimble as always, hoped to prevent misfortune. As he stepped out on the street, though, he stopped short. A blue beret—one of those—lay on the ground in its arrogance. Could it have fallen from a United Nations vehicle? Could it belong to these soldiers exercising the exclusive profession of Peace who give the world more news than tranquillity? For a few moments, Mintoninho hesitated: could he claim this find as his own, since no one had seen him? He stood twirling the beret on his indecisive fingers, dreaming up sincere uses and abuses. Then he decided: later he would hand over the hat at the Blue Berets' barracks. For now, he would just find a place for it at home.

He turned back to leave the sky-blue beret in pacific repose in the cabinet near the doorway. Then he stretched his legs on the road. But he didn't even need to get to the bar. His father was already making his way home, staggering up the sidewalk, a walking beer-sponge. Watching that figure, the boy longed for his father as he'd been before the war. As if he'd been an orphan and the man who was drawing near were a mere stepfather, a passing passerby.

The two of them, father and son, greeted each other in shared silence and walked along as if they hadn't a house in this world to call their own. And right there at the entrance, from the top of the cabinet, the blue beret seized the man with fear.

—*Who is this?*

At that moment, the entire universe couldn't contain Acubar Aboobacar. His vast shock, unleashed, overran all his nerves. The man couldn't believe what he was thinking. Could this woman, his wedded wife, have sampled new flavours among the uniformed foreigners, these witnesses to the transition from the tragedy of war to the misery of peace? To ask is shameful, to doubt is weakness. The affair demanded machismo without hesitation, ingenuity and surety. Without the light of doubt, hate flowers. At the edge of grief, suspicion took on the contours of fact. Mintoninho tried to explain to his father the reasons for the beret. But he never had a chance. His father gave his orders: the boy was to vanish immediately, like a shooting star. He should go to the veranda, there wasn't enough air inside.

Acubar Aboobacar sat there, waiting for his wife, soured by the beret in his lap. Bitter jealousy rose through his body like yeast in an oven. But it was as if he knew well the visit of this other self who, before the war, would never have lost sight of Sulima. Does jealousy make women of men?

Acubar, sitting on the floor, expected—more than his wife—the arrival of his worst fears. Death always knows where to strike us. Beret on lap, he took relief in slumber. As he slept, secrets were revealed to him. Images came to him of a fat cobra, bedecked in human garments. It donned a baby-blue capulana the colour of the United Nations and a kerchief on its head. Crawling and contorting, the animal drew closer to him and tickled him all over with its forked tongue. Snakes are bilingual to show that every animal conceals a second creature. The ophidian slipped through his legs, slithered round his waist, and slid across his chest. When it reached his neck, Acubar heard what her eyes were telling him: they were Sulima's—no more, no less. They were terrestrial, dusty, exposed eyes. They fixed upon him as opium eyes the lungs. Then, the snake spoke:

—*So it shall be, locked within one another, this is how we'll live from now on.*

Acubar felt the air flee from his chest. Closed like a paragraph, he even thought to cry out, call for help. But then, a memory came back to him, a reminiscience. The opposite of life is not death, but another dimension of existence. The serpent, it's said, was born alongside the human soul. That's right: cobras are full of deceptions, just like women. The fangs of one can be found in the mouth of the other. Sulima was extending an invitation to crawl inside him.

—*Each man's passions eviscerate his insides. I'll crawl inside you so we never have to part, flesh into flesh.*

Acubar opened his mouth, jaw-struck. Either on account of the serpent's appeal, or on account of the asphyxia that began to grip him. He woke, panting and pallid. He'd always said: When I die, it will only be to leave those absent with a yearning feeling. And now, as he felt himself grow faint, he called for his son, the most present of these absent. *Son, I'm losing my grip on life. A painful coldness is coming from my insides. It's as if there's a creature lizarding about my belly, mis-stirring up my bloods, I can't even tell if I'm dreaming it or if it's really happening.* Mintoninho took care to cover him. The father refused:

—*Leave it. Beer is my sheet.*

Then, the child watched his father transform from dermis to epidermis, as greenish-green scales appeared. It looked as though another being, monstriform, were robbing his old man of his shape. Even his voice was unrecognizable:

—*I'm no longer myself, son. It was the snake that killed me.*

—*Snake? Where?*

—*It bit me from inside. It entered here.*

At first the boy thought it was the beer talking. But then, in the face of his father's new appearance, he became worried. He wanted to go for help. But a paternal arm stopped him.

—*Leave it, son: a mouth wound is cured with one's own saliva. And it's of life I'm curing myself, of this life I didn't know how to properly enjoy.*

They say he expired at that moment, so tiny and shrunken that his son seized him in a full embrace for the very first time. That's how the boy's mother found them, statues raised in memoriam. It was strange how, barely having made sense of events, she hurriedly removed the blue beret from her husband's lap. Then, she folded it stealthily into her purse. They say.

High-Heel Shoes

It happened in colonial times. I hadn't yet reached adolescence. Life took place in Esturro, a Beira neighbourhood not lacking for neighbours. In that tiny corner, the Portuguese set down their roots. The men there never amounted to masters of anything, even their dreams suffered from a lack of ambition. Their exploring only went as far as making the rounds of neighbourly quarters. If they robbed, it was so they might never become rich. The others, the true masters, not even I knew where they lived. For certain, they didn't dwell anywhere. Dwell is a verb one applies only to the poor.

We lived in this tiny neighbourhood of dust-ridden streets, where the sun set earlier than in the rest of the city. Everything carried on there without much fanfare. Our neighbour was the only intriguing figure: an imposing, whiskered man with a voice like thunder. But friendly, a man of refinement and good manners. Everyone called him

Zé Paulão. The Portuguese man laboured at harsh altitudes at the wheel of heavy cranes. He was like a rooster with its plume of feathers hoisted high, ruler of a vast roost, but living totally alone. Other men marvelled at his aloneness, the ladies cursed at such waste. They all remarked: such a human man, a man so blessed with manliness, such a shame he was living by himself and for himself. Never did anyone witness him in the company of another. After all, God doesn't dole out nuts to just anyone.

All that was known about him was this brief summary: his wife had run away. What reasons she had for deconsummating their marriage, no one knew. She was the model modest little Portuguese woman, the daughter of humble country labourers. Beautiful, of a flowering age. We saw her only once, when she was leaving the house, fearfully white. In certain and exposed danger, she was walking down the middle of the street. The cars screeched to a stop, fishtailing. The pale white woman didn't seem to hear a thing. Then I saw: the girl was crying, a true watershed. My father stopped our vehicle and asked her how we could help. But the young woman didn't hear a thing—she was sleepwalking. My father decided to accompany the creature, protecting her from the dangers of the streets, until she disappeared where the darkness came to an end. It was only then that we were able to confirm that the woman had left the house to make a most definitive departure.

From that moment on, only solitude was capable of comforting Zé Paulão. Or so it seemed, to the neighbourly public. We, however, were the only ones who knew the truth. In the yard behind our house, where no others laid eyes, we could see, every now and then, women's clothing drying in the sun. Paulão had his ways of coping after all. But we kept our secret. My family wanted to be the only ones to relish that revelation. Let others pity the solitary man. We alone knew the backside of reality.

And there was another secret we kept to ourselves: at night, we could hear a woman's footsteps on the other side of the wall. In Zé Paulão's house, there could be no doubt, a woman's high-heel shoes ticky-tacked across the floor. They made the rounds through the bedroom, the hallway, and the sleepy rooms of our neighbour's house.

—*One hell of a scoundrel, that Paulão!*

My aunts approved of these naughty little comments, a snicker behind their teeth, their teeth covered by their hands. There was much discussion of the mysterious woman: who was it that no one ever saw arriving or departing? My mother bet: she had to be a rather tall lady, much taller than Paulão. The footsteps could only belong to a fat woman, my aunt countered. *Maybe she's so fat she can't fit through the door*, my father joked. And then, still laughing:

—*That's why we never see her leaving!*

I used to dream of her: she was the most beautiful woman in the world, so beautiful and elegant that she could only come out at night. The world's eyes didn't deserve the sight of her. Or was she an angel? Paulão, seated high up in his crane, had nabbed her by surprise. What's for certain is that the mysterious woman next door filled my dreams, ruffled my sheets, and forced me out of my own body.

One night, I took advantage of my childhood, to play little games with myself, pretending I was an adventurer, a hero from one of those shoot-em-up movies. Climbing onto the roof, I escaped the manhunt for me, outwitting hundreds of Indians below. At the last minute, I leapt to my neighbour Paulão's porch. I could even feel imaginary arrows piercing my soul. I took a deep breath and a moment to grab my plastic pistol. Then a light went on inside the house. I crouched down, fearing I'd be mistaken for a common thief. Taking a few punches at the hands of my corpulent neighbour would bring no pleasure. I hunched down into a dark corner. I could neither see nor be seen. Just then, my ears stood up. The heels. The mystery woman must have been making the rounds through the adjacent accommodations. I couldn't resist catching a glimpse. That's when I saw a woman's long skirt. I was on full alert: finally, she was right there, within eye's reach, the woman of our mysteries. There stood the woman who gave form to my desires. Indians be damned! Paulão could go to hell! I drew closer to the light, defying all concepts of prudence. Now the entire living room was within view. The fascinating lady had her back to me. She wasn't so tall in the end, nor so fat as my family had supposed. Suddenly, the woman turned around. *Thud!* The earth opened in a huge abyss. Zé Paulão's eyes, adorned with makeup, locked on me. The lights went out and I leapt from the porch, my heart catacombing into the abyss.

I returned home, my head out of tune. I locked myself in my bedroom, giving shape to the silences. Hours later, at the dinner table, the same subject returned. *Our neighbour, the immortal lover—not long ago I heard those heels over there.* It was my father who spoke, setting off a wagging of tongues. *You all are just jealous you can't do the same*, my aunt announced. Everyone laughed at once. Only I kept to myself, silently fulfilling my obligations to melancholy.

Later on, when everyone had slipped into the release of sleep, I again heard the high-heel shoes. My eyes filled with a deep, inexplicable sorrow. I was crying for what, in the end? My mother, having suspected something in that way only mothers are able, rushed into my room, filling it with light.

—*Why are you crying, my child?*

I told her about the passing of an uncertain girl whom I'd loved deeply. She'd abandoned me, betraying me with another man in the neighbourhood. My mother pretended not to understand, a stroke of her maternal wand. Her smile was filled with unusual suspicion. She tendered her fingers through my hair and said:

—*Come, come. Tomorrow you can move to another room. You'll never have to hear the sound of those high heels again.*

The Hapless Calculus of Happiness

————◆————

The man this story is about goes by the name Julio Novesfora. In certain people's mouths, Professor Novesfora. A very mathematical man, leading a life of exact quantities, always to be found in the right place. In his eyes, everything in the world was transformed into an equation to the nth degree. Algebraic operations guided his thoughts in any situation. Integers, derivatives, matrices: everything in the world had its corresponding formula. More times than not, he didn't even have to activate his neurons:

—That's an operation you can do without your head.

He also divvied out his affections in calculated doses, limiting love to its numerical equivalent. Love affairs, women, children: all those things were null hypotheses. Feelings, he was fond of saying, have no logarithm. For that reason, there was no reason to even solve the equation. Since he was a child, he'd abstained from affection. *From an algebraic point of view,* he would say, *tenderness is absurd. Like a negative zero. Look here,* he'd say to his students, *the grass doesn't find it galling to know it will meet its end at the hands of a grazing steer. And a snake bites without malice. It's just acting on its injectable impulses. In the natural world, there's no concept of feelings.* And so life went on, and Julio Novesfora waited for facts to come in.

Once, however, the professor fell for one of his students, a girl of an inappropriate age. Everyone warned him: this girl is beyond young, she isn't right for you.

—*Do the math, professor!*

But the professor had already lost count. Reasonable advice was worth nothing to him. More serious yet: he was losing his mathematical intuition. He no longer knew the basic operations. His thoughts were now void of the light of logic. He said things without stems or leaves. His case seemed to confirm the formula: more sex meant less sense. Now, reason arrived too late. The professor had already traced the hypotenuse between him and the girl. Julio Novesfora pulled back from the rigours of geometry, preferring rest and recreation. The sideways eight marks infinity. And then, the dizzoriented professor remembered once again:

—*Love is the world divided by zero.*

Let no one question his passion. His was a love without dimension, the kind for which there are no such things as oceans and wars. One of his uncles was summoned, the only family member who seemed to have earned his trust. This uncle applied all his knowledge as he made his argument, doctrines to establish facts and eliminate arguments. But the mathematician held firm:

—*If you look closely, uncle, for the first time I'm actually living. As a corollary, it's only natural for me to make errors.*

—*But, nephew, you always showed such dedication to calculus. Look at your life, you do the math.*

—*Uncle, this operation is not to be performed with the head but the heart.*

The professor made his axiom clear; there was no solution for the passion he felt for the underaged girl. He'd tasted the fruit when the summer was still performing its work on the sugars of its pulp. So infatuated was he that his eyes grew fat. He had his head packed full with the bold girl. His uncle still insisted, trotting out a series of warnings: did he not discern the danger of a disappointing denouement? Didn't he know that each enticing woman could likewise be unenticing? That love was as false as a ceiling? Be careful, nephew: an eye for an eye, a tooth for some truth. Novesfora, however, was ageless in his obstinacy. His uncle went off to live his own life.

The love affair progressed. The professor would take the young girl to the edge of the sea where the coconut trees curved, whispering in the wind, creating the impression of fresh air.

—*For a love strong and true, only the edge of the sea will do*, he recited.

The girl only responded in the simplest terms, plainspoken. What she really liked was summer.

The girl: *Winter I like for crying. In the cold, the tears flow from me in thick, full drops of water.*

The girl went on talking and Professor Novesfora passed his hands over her body with greater diligence than the blind reading braille.

—*Keep talking, don't stop*—he would walk her as his fingers danced across the girl's secret humidities. He liked when she feigned distraction, it made him feel his actions were less sinful. The passersby passed by, laying all sorts of blame at the old professor's feet. At his age? What was he, shame-nix? Others made jokes.

—*Sexagenarian or sex-o-genarian?*

The professor paid no mind. He took a lesson from the baobab, which despite its size casts no shadow. The desire to celebrate ought to appear before the dance comes to an end. So much time had already run on his clock and so little time remained to live. With everything within happiness's reach, what reason did the rest have for so seldom exercising life's joys? But a frog, after all, doesn't dream of cool ponds, it dives straight into them. Now that his hands were all over the girl, was he going to desist?

One night, when she was next to him in bed, unwelcome fears overcame the professor: this girl is going to run away, disappear like a rainbow after the rain. In the end, the others were right: the moment always arrives when the almond is separated from its shell. Novesfora couldn't so much as begin to fall asleep, so wounded was he by his premonition about his love's outcome.

Days passed. Until, once, beneath the shadow of a coconut tree, there could be heard the chords of a lament swelling from the ground. Was it the professor, wailing over his foreseen sorrows? Everyone went to see, armed with consoling words. They found not the professor but the girl spilling tears, sadder than a blind man seated before a vista. They drew closer, tapped the girl on the shoulder. What had happened? Where was the professor?

—*He left with someone else.*

A startling response, if ever there were one: after all, it was the professor who had gone away without a solution to the problem. What do you mean, he left? And why, if only yesterday he'd had his tentacles all over her in that very spot? The lucky girl responded: he left with someone else, a supernumerary. And this other girl was still younger than she was, as untouched as a Sunday morning. He who tastes unripe fruit soon wants to try its flower. As the tearful girl drowned what remained of her words, those present slowly dispersed. They forgot about it all, leaving the girl beneath the shade of the coconut tree, lonely and alone at the scene of her foretold sorrow. Winter had arrived, her favourite season for shedding tears.

Joãotónio, For Now

For now, I'm Joãotónio. I'll say it and then I'll unsay it: when it comes to women, I advance like the army. 'Cause my whole encounter with them feels like a battle. What I mean is the minute I look at a woman, I already start wondering: what's her voice like? It's not her audible voice that piques my interest, but the other, silent one, disembodied, capable of speaking as many languages as water. In other words: what I want to decipher are their moans, these wings sliding to the edge of the abyss, the chill that runs up the soul when it's lost its home.

You know what I'm talking about, Bro: a person's voice obscures the sweet taste of her sighing. The voice conceals the way she sighs. I can already hear your question: what's this obsession with unravelling the secrets behind the way a woman sighs? It's the same desire a general has, Bro. It's the taste of the enemy's surrender. It's the desire to hear in advance the way they make love, subdued and abandoned.

Sometimes, I stop to think: deep down, I'm afraid of women. Aren't you? You are, I'm sure of it. Their thoughts come from a place that's beyond reason. That's where our fear comes in: we're unable to make sense of their way of thinking. Their superiority frightens the hell out of us, Bro. That's why we see them as well-versed adversaries in a battle. But let me get back to the beginning—just look at me, screeching like a hairpin turn, swerveering off into this pseudo-philosophizing. And start your listening over, too.

For the time being, I'm still Joãotónio. What I'm telling you now is the fiction of my unhappiness. Don't go telling this to everyone. I'm trusting you, Bro. 'Cause it's not just anyone who makes his troubles public. What I'm about to write is cause for shame.

I'll start with Maria Zeitona, source of all urges. As I write the name of this woman, I can still hear her voice, smooth as a bird's wings. I already told you: a woman's voice is as important as her body. It whets the appetite more than appearances or seductions ever could, at least for me.

As I wasn't saying: Maria Zeitona seemed to be intact and untouchable. She gave off suspicion like an ember beneath ashes. Her body spoke through her eyes. And what crystalluminous eyes! We were married in an instant. I wanted nothing more than to suffer the promise of that inferno. I was marrying to consummate the ardencies swarming 'round my dreams. But the bad news, my brother: Maria Zeitona was ice cold, frigelid! It was as if I were making love to a corpse. You could say we maintained asexual relations. And that's how she stayed more virgin than Mother Mary. I tried, I tried again, I used every technique from the whole of my experience. All the same, Bro: for nothing. Zeitona was damp firewood: flames could not touch her.

I changed tactics, I gave her worthy surprises. I ran through all the preliminaries I knew. I even kissed the tips of her toes. Still no luck. A kiss is neither given nor received. It's life that does the kissing, and the kissing back. I'll say it again, Bro: it's life that kisses us, two beings in an infinite moment. Enough with the family chat? All right, got it, Bro, I'll get back to this subject of mine, Maria Zeitona.

At the end of these campaigns, I gave her a penultimatum: either she sweetened up or I'd resort to unfortunate measures. And that's what didn't happen. That, Bro, is when I made my decision: I'd send Zeitona to a prostitute. That's right, my little Zeitona would intern with a pro of the romp and raze. That's how she'd learn to tangle in the sheets. At last she'd commit immortal sin.

It didn't take long for me to find the right instructor: it would be Maria Mercante, the renowned Bacchanalian, with an innate talent for horizontal acts. Dark-skinned, deep-dipped black. Possessor of savoury fillings. In this world, there are two creatures that use their rear to get ahead in life: the wild boar and Maria Mercante. I got straight to the point with that piece of tail:

—*Please, give my wife a lesson in nuptial twistings and turnings!*

—*Rest assured, sir. It's no use for a woman to be known for her qualities: she needs to have qualifications!*

And the able prostitute got to work. She held forth on irrelevant subjects—perhaps just to increase the price of these lessons. Zeitona would leave virginity behind with more regrets than the only one to have conceived without sin. Zeitona knew the math: the Virgin Mary had, in the end, turned down the visit of the Holy Spirit. She'd responded in these terms: *Bear a child without making love? Where's the pleasure in that? Go without food but get stuck belching anyway? I'll teach Zeitona. None of these platonics: sex at first sight.*

I interrupted her, directing the conversation to my more material woes. Advanced payment guaranteed, Maria Mercante accepted the job. I could rest assured: my wife would leave her tutelage hotter than the midday sun. We'd ruffle the sheets until the mattress begged for urgent repairs. And off Zeitona went to this place of ill repute. We might as well say it: an undressing room.

Weeks passed. The course ended, my wife came back home. She was, indeed, a changed woman. She had a different way about her but not in the way I'd expected. Man, I'm almost ashamed to admit it: all of a sudden my little Zeitona came on like a man! She, who usually sat back on her heels, was now leading the charge! That is and was: my Zeitona oozed manlihood. And not just when making love. The entire time, in everything she did. Her voice, even. Everything in her had changed, Bro, to the point I had to scratch my male parts just to be sure they were still there. I'm telling you: she was the one who pushed me to the bed—you better believe it. She's the one who turned me on, took my breath away. I lay there like a spectator, commanded and directed like a girl during her first time. And it's that way to this day.

The problem, Bro, is this: I kinda like it. It's tough for me to admit it, so much so that I hesitate to write this. But the truth is that I'm enjoying this new position of mine, my era of passive initiate, being on the bottom, the embarassment, the fear.

That's it, Bro. Explain it to me, if you can. I don't know what to think. At first, I would make excuses: after all, there are several versions of the truth that can claim to be truthful. For example: when it comes to sex, there's no male-female. The two lovers join into a single, binary being. There was no reason to think I'd been given a lower position. You following, my brother?

But now, at the moment I write, I no longer have any appetite for explanations. Only for unreason. Every day the one thing I look forward to is nighttime, the quiet storms when I become Joãotónio and Joanantónia, man and woman, in my wife's virile arms. But for now, Bro, I'm still Joãotónio. I'm saying goodbye, meanderly, to my real name.

That Devil of an Advocate

The attorney rested his patience in the palm of his hand. Time was stretching on, the consultation had already exceeded its actual worth. He turned his head back to the woman seated in front of him. He'd stopped listening to her minutes ago. His distraction focused on the woman's legs, which she crossed and uncrossed. They had too much flesh for so little clothing. Resigned, the advocate returned to his duties as listener. The woman put forth her reasons for having left her husband.

—*My husband snores.*

—*And that's a reason? There are more people in the world snoring than sleeping.*

—*Yes, mister attorney, sir. But this husband of mine snores backward.*

—*Snores backward?*

—*Yeah, he only snores when he's awake.*

The attorney thought to himself: here is a woman of piss and vinegar. And he asked for more information, a firmer foundation. But his client continually wandered back to a story as useless as glasses in the hands of a blind man.

—*Now you look closely at me here, sir. You think I've gone senile? No, no—you don't have to answer that. The answer is clear as can be, it's in your eyes, mister attorney, sir. But this husband of mine is a big old soul. If you'd only seen him: towering, broad-reaching. But only from the neck up. Because on the lower levels, from the waist down…*

—*I'm sorry, Miss. But these details…*

—*Details? It's exactly these details that result in children! You'll excuse me for saying so, sir, but you, sir, were born on account of a detail, mister attorney, sir… Intimacy doesn't intimidate me. We only call it trash because the smell twists our nostrils. But getting back to my husband, before the trail goes cold. If only you knew what a little Casanova he was. Night never fell, mister attorney, sir. How did he become like this? I've spent years asking myself, mister attorney, sir. You know what he says? That I don't turn him on because I spend my whole life crying. Now you tell me, is that a reason? Sure, it's true, I really do enjoy a good cry. I can't go a single day without spilling a little bit. But, for him, my former-ex-husband, this never used to be a problem. Before, he would clamber all over me, he never once slipped on my tears. It's only recently that he stopped visiting my body. And you know why?*

*You know why he suddenly stopped? It was because he kissed
me with his eyes closed. Yes, that's it, he would kiss me with
his eyes shut tight. You, mister attorney, sir, you'll forgive the
intrusion, but how is it that you kiss?*

—*How do I kiss? What sort of question…*

—*Don't tell me that you haven't been kissing, mister attorney, sir… Don't respond if you don't want to. But you, sir, know
as well as anybody: a man can't ever kiss with his eyes closed.*

—*I know what it is they say about this, that you lose your way
and your soul, that sort of thing… But I don't worry about such
things. In fact, I don't close my eyes.*

—*And don't you ever start, mister attorney, sir. If you do,
there's no way back.*

The doctor of jurisprudence turned his attention back to
the elegance with which the woman crossed and uncrossed
her legs in her chair. The woman, all of a sudden, grew quiet.
And stayed that way, on pause. Later, she scooted her chair
closer to him and whispered:

—*Now, mister attorney, sir. Don't you start covering for my
husband. Don't be a devil of an advocate…*

—*It's backward, miss.*

—*Backward? We'll see about that later. You know something, mister attorney sir, I've been watching your eyes. Do you
cry much, sir?*

—*Me? Cry?*

—*Yes, there's no shame in it. Tell me.*

And, having said this, she got up from her seat and sat on his desk. Her knees brushed up against the responsible attorney. The woman passed her fingers along his face and said:

—*I'll bet you don't know how to have a proper cry, doctor. There's a certain technique to it, you know. I'm quite an expert on the subject. I'm a graduate in sadnesses, I've done all the coursework. Suffering—what's suffering? Suffering is a road: you walk along it, forward along its endless distance, to reach another side. This other side is a part of ourselves that we've never known. I, for example, I've already travelled far and wide within myself...*

The woman hopped down off the desk and made a spot for herself on the attorney's lap. The man, knowing he was in the wrong, didn't do a thing. He seemed to abandon himself to her. The woman continued her advances.

—*I'm going to give you a crash course in crying. Don't make that face. Men cry, yes, they do. They just have their own way of doing it. I'm going to teach you how to get the tears flowing.*

—*But, miss, in all honesty...*

—*In all honesty, in all honesty. Listen up, learn something. There's no reason to be ashamed. First, do the following: gather up not that most recent and justified reason for sadness. It's not healthy to cry out each heartache one at a time. Each time we cry, we need to cry over every heartache from every life we've ever lived. We have to summon old wounds, bundle together every disappointment we've ever had. As if we were constructing a dike, to stop the flow of water. Here, see what I mean? Let me rest my hand on your chest. Come on. Unbutton your shirt, mister attorney, sir. Yes, right here. This is where all the rivers and their tributaries are going to swell until there's a flood. Suddenly, you're going to see, mister attorney, sir: everything bursts and the waters gush forth. Crying is a moment of torrid passion: when we finish, we're tired, like our bodies after making love.*

The well-behaved lawman had already lain down lower than the sunset. His tie, unhoisted, danced in his client's hand. Inexplicably, one of his client's shoes rested atop the computer. The woman saw to the jurist's horizonality.

—*Tell me, mister attorney, sir: would you like to cry with me now? Now, there's no reason to be afraid. And there's another, second commandment in the sobbing arts. You should never cry alone. It's very bad, it's harmful to your sadness. Crying alone invites evil spirits. If you want to shed a tear then cry together with someone else, two souls in tune.*

She pulled his face toward her half-bared breasts. She herself unbuttoned her shirt even further. She felt the attorney's damp lips on her breast. But more than that, she felt his tears, abundant waters flowing forth. His tears were so large that they tingled as they ran down her body, tickling her. The two of them proceeded to follow the law that demanded that each body be a cup: turn it over and it spills across the floor. The two of them, were their lives to end at that moment, could be said to be not in an immoral but an immortal position.

And that's the scene to which, to her great shock, the attorney's secretary opened his office door. The jurist and his client, in each other's arms, the two of them spilling tears everywhere. Why they were gushing tears as though a dam had broken, the secretary didn't understand. What astounded her most was seeing the way the doctor kissed: his eyes shut, closed tighter than the door the secretary shut to separate herself from that shocking scene.

War of the Clowns

One time, two clowns began to argue. The people would stop, amused, to watch them.

—*What's that?* they asked.

—*Why, it's only two clowns arguing.*

Who could take them seriously? Ridiculous, the two comedians retorted. The arguments were common nonsense, the theme was a ninnery. And an entire day passed.

The following morning, the two remained, obnoxious and outdoing each other. It seemed as though, between them, even yucca soured. In the street, meanwhile, those present were exhilarated by the masquerade. The buffoons began sharpening their insults with fine-edged and fine-tuned barbs. Believing it to be a show, the passers-by left coins along the roadside.

On the third day, however, the clowns resorted to violence. Their blows were clumsy, their counter-kicks zinged more across air than across bodies. The children rollicked, imitating each jester's blows. And they laughed at the two fools, their bodies tripping upon their own selves. And the boys wanted to repay the delightful generosity of the clowns.

—*Dad, give me some coins to leave on the sidewalk.*

On the fourth day, the jabs and blows grew worse. Beneath their makeup, the faces of the clowns began to bleed. Some kids became scared. Was that real blood?

—*It's not serious, don't fret,* their parents soothed them.

Missed aims resulted in some being struck by blows. But it was light fare, only serving to add to the laughs. More and more people joined the gallery.

—*What's going on?*

Nothing. A friendly unsettling of accounts. It's not worth separating them. They'll tire themselves out, it's nothing more than a bit of clowning around.

On the fifth day, however, one of the clowns armed himself with a stick. Advancing on his adversary, he discharged a blow that tore off his wig. The other, furious, equipped himself with an identical truncheon and responded with the same lack of proportion. The wooden rods whistled through the air in somersaults and deliriums. One of the spectators, unexpectedly, was struck. The man fell, deadspread.

A certain confusion arose; the supporters divided into two camps. Little by little, two battlefields began to form. Various groups traded punches. Still more lay fallen.

The quarrel entered a second week and in the surrounding neighbourhoods it was heard said that a dizzied pandemonium had set in around the two clowns. And the thing embroiled the entire plaza. And the neighbours found it funny. Some went to the plaza to verify the reports. They returned with contradicting and inflamed versions of their own. The neighbourhood continued to divide itself, in opposing opinions. Conflicts began in other neighbourhoods.

On the twentieth day, shots could be heard. No one knew exactly where they came from. It could have been from any point in the city. Full of terror, the inhabitants armed themselves. The tiniest movement seemed suspect. The gunshots spread. Dead bodies began to pile up in the streets. Terror reigned over the whole city. Soon, massacres ensued.

At the beginning of the month, all the city's inhabitants had died. All except the two clowns. That morning, the comics sat, each one in his corner, and cast off their ridiculous dress. They looked at each other, worn out. Later, they rose to their feet and embraced, laughing at the flags dispersed along the ground. Arm in arm, they gathered the coins from the roadsides. Together they crossed the destroyed city, careful not to tread on the corpses. And they went in search of another city.

Legend of Namaroi

(Inspired by the report of the wife to the local
ruler, as told to Father Elia Ciscato)

I'm going to tell you the story of the world, the reason men and women burst to life. I took advantage of my illness to receive this wisdom. What I'm about to tell you was communicated to me by our ancestors in a dream. Were it not for this, I'd never be able to tell you this. I'm a woman, I need permission to speak. The things I tell you now are things I never knew. In this fever heat, those responsible for our existence and who give and take our names from us now speak with my tongue. Now, you, sir: translate my words without delay. It won't be long before I lose this voice that's come my way.

In the beginning, we were all women. Men were nowhere to be found. And so it continued until a group of women appeared who were unable to give birth. They would become pregnant but did not return the seed they carried with them to the world. Then the following happened: the remaining women grabbed hold of the infertile ones and swallowed them completely whole. For three days they remained full with these loads, made round by this new pregnancy. After this time, the women who had swallowed the others gave birth. Those beings who were inside wombs returned but as others, never before seen. The first men were born. These new creatures looked at their progenitors and were ashamed. They felt they were different, taking up new behaviours and picking fights. The men decided to seek out a new ground.

They crossed the brook and emigrated to the other side of Mount Namuli. As soon as they settled in this new land, they saw that the thread of water grew. The brook soon became a stream, the stream a river. On the bank where they had settled, the men ate only raw food. And so they would remain for ages. One evening they saw, from the other side, the flicker of bonfires. The women knew how to harvest the flame, they sowed flames like those versed in the arts of the seed and the sickle. The men remarked:

—*The women have a red spot: it's from there the fire blazes.*

Then, the *mwene* who ruled the men sent them to seek the light and bring it to him intact. Two men forded the river to execute his command. But they were unable to fulfill their duty: the flames spilled forth and evaporated. The fire was unable to cross the river.

—*The water's putting out the fire,* mwene.

This is what they told the *mwene*. Disillusioned, the chief took the mission upon himself. He waded across the current on a night of heavy rain. The river tide was rising, tempestuous. The *mwene* shed his body, allowing his soul to escape. He awoke on the other bank, wetter than a fish. He felt himself being tugged, given air and new life. Then he saw a woman, who came to his aid, lighting a tiny fire to dry his clothes. The man spoke to her, confessing his desires, his envies and intentions. The woman said:

—*Fire is a river. You must harvest it at the source.*

—*This source: we do not know its home.*

It was night. The woman called the *mwene* and made him lie against the earth. And then she covered herself with him, his body wrapped with another body as its sheet. No man had ever slept with the women from the other bank. The woman, in the end, kissed his eyes, leaving the taste of a drop of water. It was a tear of blood, a wound from the earth. The tear wailed and howled, imploring them to once again sew together the two banks that had been opened in its flesh. His hand drowsed over her smooth abyss.

Tucked up against the woman's breast, the man unfurled a dream: he was the last man on earth. And during the tangling of bodies that he'd experienced only that night he'd wounded himself, his body torn open, an emptied vein. He watched the blood spread through the river and lost consciousness. When he came to, he stood by as all of the river's water turned to blood. He followed the course of the river and noted the red thickening, transforming into a clot, the clot becoming solid. A human form taking shape. Little by little, a woman was born. And, at that instant, the river began to flow again, its waters pure and limpid. This was his dream. The dream the *mwene* forgot even before he woke.

The chief awoke and returned to the other bank. As he crossed, he saw that the river had grown placid, its waters peaceful in a way never before seen. The man reached the others, as restless as if he'd unlearned how to breathe. The others stared at him with astonishment. Did he carry a flame inside himself? The *mwene* was still seeking his wind:

—*Listen, there on the other side...*

And with that, he collapsed. The others set out, propelled by the itch to know for themselves. They left after the sun hid itself. Each time one of them returned, the river slowed to a trickle, more like a stream. As it turned out, there was an unknown side to the night, the other side of life. In the end, the river current returned to what it had been: a tiny, bashful little trickle. The world was no longer separated into two sides. The men, little by little, decided to join the domain of women. On the other, old bank, not a single man remained.

Time passed. One day a woman gave birth. The men flew into a frenzy: they'd never witnessed a child being born. The pregnant woman went behind the house and joined the other women, and they cut the child where he merged with the mother. The cord cut, what was one became two, the blood separating the bodies as the river had split the earth before.

The men saw this and murmured: if the women can wield knives then we can, too. They sharpened their knives and took the young boys to the forest. And so began circumcision. They cut their sons so that upon entering the world they might forget the other bank, from whence the first men had come. And the men felt consoled: they could, at least, give a second birth. And so they deceived themselves into thinking they had powers equal to those of the women: they gave life as much as the women did. They were mistaken: only women cut the tie between one life and the next. We let it go, we don't even bother seeking to convince them otherwise. Because after all, to this day they continue to cross the river current to seek in us the source of their flame.

The Woman Engulfed in Stone

I'm no man of the church. I find it impossible to believe and this causes me distress. Because after all, I hold within me all the religiosity one could ask of any believer. I'm religious without religion. I suffer, you'd have to say, from a condition called poetry: I dream up places where I've never set foot, I believe only in that which cannot be proven. And even if I were to pray today, I wouldn't know what to ask of God. This is my fear: only the mad don't know what to ask of God. Or is it possible that God has lost faith in man? Anyway, my appetite for visiting churches comes only from the tranquilitude of these small vaulted spaces, filled with soothing shadows. Here, I'm able to breathe. Outside, the world awaits with its unresolved calamities.

It was on one of these visits that something happened that I can't help but recall. The tiny church was made of raw stone, rock that's as old as the earth. It didn't even seem like the work of man. I took in the statues of the saints, made of wood and with so much soul you could feel it. That's when I heard some kittens. At first, I doubted my ears. The sounds I heard resembled nothing on this earth. Was I being summoned by forces from beyond? I quivered at the thought. Who's ever prepared to address eternity? The hissing continued and, then, I made her out: there was an old woman calling to me. She was half-covered by a stone column. She prayed with her entire body, hunched over with the humility of one who asks more than she is owed. I again heard her weak murmurs.

—*Psst, psst.*

—*Me?*

—*Yes. You there. Help me up.*

I tried to help her up. I failed. Not even I expected such tonnage from that tiny creature. I tugged again. Not a single inch of her budged. The old woman could not get to her feet. Her kneecaps were glued to the ground, she was unable to stand. She asked me for help in the form of a hand and a lift. Me, who suffers from aching bones, rheumasthmatic. A tiny piece of paper of less than twenty-five lines, for me, is already a heavy weight. What to do? I sat down next to the old woman, hesitating over how to grab on to her.

—*Come on, help pull me up from the floor. Quick, young man, I've begun to turn to stone.*

I tried again to get a grip on her body. Hers was an inert weight, its gravity stronger than a planet's.

—*Don't scrunch up my dress. It came from the disasters. I came by this dress with the priests.*

I tried again, made fresh attempts: the old lady remained stuck to the floor. She didn't move a fraction of a millimetre. Could she be making fun of me? How could a body as slim as this one weigh so much? I thought of calling for help. But there was no one else to call.

—*Hold on: I'm going to fetch someone else.*

—*Don't leave me alone, young man. Don't leave me, please.*

I looked around. The tiny church was empty. I circled the area, entered the sacristy. Not a soul. I went back to tell the old woman I would call someone from outside. The woman grabbed me by the hands, with fevered fervour.

—*Outside, no. Don't go out there. Try one more time, just one more time.*

Yet again, I made fresh attempts, I redoubled my efforts. The old lady didn't budge a centimetre. Suddenly, there was the slam of a door. I peered through the shadows. The heavy doors of the church had shut. I ran towards them much too late. I cried out, shouted, beat my hands against them. In vain. I tried breaking down the door; the old lady dissuaded me. It was worse than a mortal sin to damage the House of God.

—*But we need to get out, we can't stay stuck in here.*

However, the door was bust-proof. The pious woman and I were prisoners of the dark. I lit all the candles I could find and sat down next to her. I listened to her ramblings: *Do you know, young man, do you know what I was just asking God? I was asking him to take me, my hut up above is all ready and waiting. And here I am, suffering like this! Problem is, I no longer have the body to ascend to heaven alone. I'm so old, so awfully tired that I can't handle climbing all those steps till I reach the beyond. You know what I asked? I asked God to make me into a bird, one of the ones that fly long distances, the kind that fly and fly until they've passed beyond infinity. It's true, young man. This afternoon, I asked God to make me a bird. And to grant me wings to take me from this world.*

I fell asleep during all her tongue-twisting. I fell into a deep sleep, like the rock I'd laid my head upon. I was totally out of it, in the absence of noise, of the groans and clamours of the city. I woke the next day, shaken by a priest. What was I doing there, sleeping about like a filching duck-thief? I began to explain about the old lady.

—*What old lady?* the clergyman asked.

I looked around. There was not even a wisp of the old woman. Wasn't there a woman here with her knees glued to the floor? The priest, a man of impatient patience, asked me to leave. And not to continue making improper use of the holy place. I went out, downjected. Behind the door, the world was a thing to behold, a salve for unhealed wounds. The morning light had me seeing stars. Nothing's so blinding as the sun.

In my muddledness came a sudden vision of a huge, white bird. Right before my eyes, right there, the bird darted off course, weaving in and out between dirt and leaves. I waved, a bit awkward, bowled over. She gave me a smile: *What are you doing, saying goodbye? No, I'm not going over to any other side. This request of God, it was a lie. Oh, did I pull one over on him. I have no desire to climb up there, toward the eternities. I want to be a bird to soar through life. I want to travel in the world. And this world, young man, isn't to be abandoned for anything on earth.*

Then she lifted off in flights of fancy.

Drinking the Time By

That afternoon, I'd sat down on the sidewalk to gather peace into my bereft soul. At a pause in my voyage, I was waiting to return to the capital. In that passing village, quite far north, the heat bore down. Contact with the air was enough to strip people there of their youth. The truth is, I was becoming airsfixiated. I'd chosen to sit outside in the hope of getting some refreshment. The bar was called Hell's Bellows and worthy of the name. I sat there, watching with pleasure as young women sauntered by, the kind who have more grace than dragonflies that make love while suspended in flight. Until I saw a swarthy man, playing cards, a few tables away. Not appearing to be in his right mind, the guy was waving his arms in the air, generating both sweat and attention. I asked what he was doing, but the others demanded that I show respectful silence.

—*Quiet there! This here is Xidakwa. He's embracing God.*

The living are always disappearing. Xidakwa! The man was from the town of my birth, a career drunk, a subject with a long, sud-soaked resumé. What was he doing so far from his hometown? I drew closer in the vain hope of being recognized. Layers of misty confusion dulled his eyes. At last, he strung together a coherent sentence.

—*I'm sorry, I forgot my name.*

Turning to the crowd, he asked, *Someone call my name, please...*

Life is water hardening up stone. After all, what it requires is strength of spirit. I helped the inebriated man back to his seat. I filled his glass with what remained of my bottle. Did he remember our shared hometown, back in the days of yesteryear? He made a declaration, pointing to the bar.

—*This place, this bar, is my home!*

And there he stayed, all morning long. One by one, the man paid his respects to the bottles before him. At day's end, the bar's owner filled me in. One day long ago, this man from my hometown had arrived and set up there, as though he'd definitely inherited the spot. Any time they asked him for an explanation, Xidakwa would begin to explain, with dis-purpose:

—*I'm waiting on a certain woman, one too good for this world.*

—*What about all this drinking?* they dared to wonder.

—*I'm not drinking beer. I'm drinking the time by, to see if she doesn't show up.*

In the beginning, the bar owner made a point of complaining. But later, he realized he could use the situation to his advantage. The drunk man helped to spread word to the surrounding areas. His presence brought the bar a new clientele. And after all, every dot in time implies a hint of the future: someone would turn up in the end, a relative or a friend, to pay the man's mounting expenses.

And in fact, one day Xidakwa's wife, kids and even a brother-in-law came. They begged, cried, and implored. Wouldn't he come back home where he belonged? They showered him with never-ending affections. It was pointless. Distrustful, the man offered but a single response.

—*I know you—you all are the type that no sooner look at a lion than you think to find a cage.*

His dejected family soon lost any hope for him. Before they left, the bar owner went to speak with the man's brother-in-law. Who would pay Xidakwa's past and future expenses? The in-law washed his hands, his bracelets, and his rings. The barkeeper decided he'd evict the drunk. He would let the man sleep there one last night, the end of the line for his complaisance.

But then something unexpected happened: as if the South weren't the only place where calculations and statistics faltered. That same night, gunmen entered the village, carrying out an armed robbery. The villagers, without exception, fled to the forest. Leaving everything behind, their possessions and belongings. The village stood deserted. One man, Xidakwa, stayed behind, in his own far-off fog. The criminals surrounded the bar, ready to plunge a knife into the ribs of the unsuspecting drunkard. Sensing the approaching shadows, Xidakwa raised his bottle, pointing it to the sky. He wished to make an offering of kindness, to welcome these recent arrivals. Then a voice from one of the assailants let out a warning.

—*The guy is armed!*

There was an exchange of mortal gunfire. One of the assailants dropped, at once, a hole through the target right between his eyes. The remaining crooks panicked, beating a chaotic retreat. The next morning, the townspeople declared Xidakwa, good old Xidakwa, a fearless hero of great courage. Moreover, they nicknamed him the drunk diviner. The news spread that he could divine the future, that he knew the unknowable. From then on, people came to ask his advice and counsel. As he received the afflicted, the man would send for more beer. His eyes spun in their sockets, unable to spell out a prediction. He always proffered the same prediction, confusing his words.

—*From this day forward…*

And nothing more. He would slump back into his chair, round as a planet. His prophecies were nothing if not fantasies of silence. All the same, the townspeople rewarded him with their faith. What his words did not say, the good people made up for with bits of imputed wisdom. The gods, after all, have no use for clear explanations.

But the drinking man, it was plain to see, had long since lost heart. He became gaunt, right before their soppy eyes. He was wilting away. He no longer drank. He'd order up a bottle and sit there eyeing it in passive contemplation. The drinking man fell ill, his liver quarrelling with his insides. The Portuguese doctor arrived, in a lightning visit. This was his diagnosis: Xidakwa was hanging on by a sud, he had but a few more days.

That's what the bar owner told me, as night came around the corner. The following morning, I awoke feeling different about Xidakwa, as if we'd shared our eve of execution. I set off toward the bar, of a mind to share urgent memories with him. I wanted to learn how to drink the time away, each drop an age gone by. I went to the bar, looked inside and out. But Xidakwa was nowhere to be seen, there was no seat where he could be found.

—Didn't you hear?

The bar owner recounted what everyone had seen. At some point during the night an unknown woman had arrived, sent by whom or from where nobody knew. They say—doubt it if you like—she was the colour of corn, a yellowish tone. It was confirmed and verified that the lady took a seat at the same table as Xidakwa. And that with tremulous tenderness, he asked her for a little time more, he only needed one more, the very last glass. The woman smiled. Then she took the drunkard by his hands and, slowly and incredibly, began to lead Xidakwa inside the glass. Do the math yourself—it doesn't make sense: the man who'd sought refuge inside this remote bar was migrating toward liquid eternity, inside his own beer.

I sat down, overcome by who knows what feeling. I began to order beers, one bottle after the next. I went on drinking, slowly, savouring with each gulp the wandering palate of time. In the mid-afternoon, some men came to warn me that the van to take me home was making its very last call. I made some vague gesture, not understanding. When night arrived, the bar owner came to let me know that it was closing time. I'm staying, I told him, feeling like I'd arrived home:

—*I am waiting for someone…*

The Deaf Father

I write like God: to the point but without straight lines. Let whoever reads my words disentangle them. Only death is straightforward. Everything else has two degrees of doubt. Like me, a product of mixed lineage. My father, a Portuguese, light hair and light eyes. My mother was black, black as coal. And so I was born with little shading in my skin but deep hues in my soul.

I speak of God with respect but without faith. As a boy, I never entered a church, not even to be baptized. That's my father's fault. Praying, he used to say, only serves to wear out pant legs. His skepticism told him that the church was an unhealthy place.

— *You barely walk inside, take two steps, and you're supposed to fall on your knees?*

At school, the priest's pointer singled me out: this must be the rain child. He never shows up at catechism and no doctrine has ever sunk in. He advised the other children to keep their distance.

—Bad apples should be plucked from the bunch.

They followed his advice and steered clear of me. Today I know that it wasn't out of obedience to the priest. I was alone on account of my colour. Like the word of God blotted by the rain. Yes, the teacher was right: I was a rain child.

And it's in the rain that I now look back upon my life. Each and every time, I begin with the blast that rattled my childhood. The bomb came wrapped in a book of postcards, and exploded as though tearing open the world. No blood was shed, save for mine. Scalding threads reeled down my neck. I wiped my face in search of the source. I discovered only with great effort: the blood had burst forth from my body, through my ears.

With all the commotion, no one bothered to notice me. There were cries, flames, my brothers. Days later, I complained about the buzzing: only then did they notice I'd stopped hearing. My ears were put to rest.

My mother blamed my old man. He'd been playing with fire, on account of addiction to kindness. We fled that town as if it were cursed, far beyond the world I'd known. My father feared more violence was yet to break out, wars born of the politics of those times.

Ever since, I've lost my reasons to enjoy life. The other children would play blind man's bluff. But what role could I play? Only the deaf man. In the beginning, I still could make out the shadows of sounds, the edges of sound-scratches. As I grew older, however, things became worse and, after some time, even the walls could hear better than I did.

Recognizing my handicap took some time. I was like a cripple convinced it's the world that's off-kilter.

—*Ah, so it's not you who's deaf? It's the entire world, then, that's mute?*

No one could convince me otherwise. Only the silence. I can't even describe this hollow abyss, this labyrinth of nothing. On I went, filling up with anguish, lone and lonely. And then one day, I'd come undone, at wit's end.

—*Dad: bring me a girl.*

I asked nearly voiceless. My father tried to toy around, but seeing the depth of my sadness, he took me by the hand.

—*Do you want to get married?*

I had read his lips, but acted as if I hadn't understood. He lowered his eyes, embarrassed. Did the girl I longed for exist?

—*I only want someone to listen to, Dad.*

I'd touched the man to his core. My father called local officials, appealed to tribal leaders, promised certain monies in return. For days, the search covered side roads and far-flung villages. Even today, I don't understand what guided their search, without so much as an image of this girl I longed for. Later, tired of looking, the scouts returned.

—*We found all sorts of girls. But this girl, the one he's looking for, we couldn't even catch a glimpse.*

Until one day they brought a girl of rare beauty to our house. She was, however, mute. My father turned her away, mindful of my request. Greater even than the desire to feel another's caress was my desire to hear another voice. They were about to turn the girl away when I appeared. I called to her and, in fear, she drew closer. I confessed my desire. My father tried to interrupt the entire time, aware of the girl's unimaginable voice. But lacking the heart to reveal her handicap. I took the visitor by the hands and asked her:

—I only want you to tell me: where can I listen to the eagle's cry?

The young girl whispered a secret. In reality, today I know that not a single audible word came from her mouth. But at the time, I basked in the illusion of her voice. My father looked on, caught by surprise, as my expression changed. I unbudded, deblossoming. Is it a miracle that in this world there aren't more miracles?

The girl was sent to the back room, where she was to spend the night. My heart was in such turmoil that no rest visited me. The next morning, my mother called me and, with gestures, explained herself.

—The girl—we sent her away.

—Away?

—She's very dark, she's blacker than black. Look at you: a mixed boy, nearly white. We can't set our family back.

My father tried to calm things down: the girl's throat was maimed, she couldn't so much as grunt a vowel. But I'd already settled on a different fate. What did I do? I feigned I was a priest. I needed nothing more than to swipe a frock and cross. Then I hid in the forest, put the town far behind me, and reached the last bend in the horizon.

There was no place—on any map—more remote. The town was called NoWhere. I dedicated myself to rebuilding a tiny parish that already existed. In any event, there'd been another priest there before me, a man of generosity, who'd filled his pews with multitudes. An extra coincidence: like me, he, too, had been deaf. The result being that the people there believed deafness to be a prerequisite for the office of country priest. Now, thinking back on what I did, even I must admit: the devil must be equipped with a terrible memory. There are so many things he can't remember.

In passing myself off as a man of the cloth, I'd discovered a way to live off the kindness of others. They looked after me, furnished the necessities. The poor folks—I made up prayers they found difficult to recite. Because with each recitation, I changed the words. Yet not even this caused the bewildered believers to waver in their convictions. Who knows, maybe it was my dedication to everything that, before, I'd never known. Nursing? I did that. Teaching? I gave it a try. Offering advice? I gave that a shot, too. In the end, in everything I did, I embodied kindness. Who knows if, as a result of having performed all these jobs, I filled the pews. On infallible Sundays, people poured in from the countryside to confess their sins.

They themselves were serious. Only I stole the sacred stage. I'd sit in the confessional, dark as a turtle's belly. One by one, the faithful kneeled outside the confessional and, at the top of their lungs, confessed their sins. In so doing, they knew what was in each other's hearts. That's how my predecessor had done things, and so it continued with me.

Yesterday, it rained so hard that the surrounding huts shook, threatening to collapse. The people came, seeking refuge in the church. At no other Mass had I ever seen so many. And then, from among the drenched villagers, I spotted a young woman, the very same girl my father had sent for to console me. Time had etched her face, her body. Each stroke to beauty's benefit. She concentrated on me with those same eyes that had turned me to a fool on my childhood porch. Then she went off in search of the heat of the fireplace. I thought I saw her talking to the others, coming to some agreement, exchanging words. I called the sexton over and gave him orders.

—*That woman over there. Go and see if she can speak.*

My assistant understood nothing at first. Off he went, getting closer and closer to her. He made a sign confirming that yes indeed, the woman plainly spoke. I was struck, a match lit in a volcano. My entire life came before me, in broken pieces, as if a bomb were shattering my memory. I climbed the altar, signalled for the dozens there assembled to quiet down. I know how to spot silence, I can read its arrival. I detect it in people's eyes. I knew, at that moment: only the rain could be heard, tim-tim-ba-tinning on the roof of the tiny church. Then, I told them what I'm committing to paper now, the tenor of my dishonesty, my fake vestures, my apocryphal prayers. I confessed aloud, as they had done before me. I removed my frock, said my goodbyes, and left, making my way past unbelieving eyes.

Outside, as I'd surmised, the rain came down. My head spun, I hadn't realized how hard it was raining. Did the heavens threaten a flood? I took a few drunkard's steps seeking the ground beneath the pools of water. Is it the blind man who never falters? A hand grabbed hold of me and turned me around. It was a young woman, that young woman. When she spoke, I lost my bearings completely. Will you believe me, now knowing of my treachery? Who do I swear to if I've lost even my ties to God? In other words, go ahead and doubt. But I heard her voice, indeed, I heard her without reading her lips. I listened to the woman's gentle voice, her words wrapping me in my own alarm.

—*Stay—please stay… dear Father!*

The Oracle of Death

In the tiny neighbourhood of Muitetecate there was a power-ful spiritualist who could predict, with algebraic accuracy, the day of a person's death. He made no use of the conventional methods: stones, shells, tiny bones. No—he had two small ivory crosses that he laid over the eyes of those who came for a consultation. The oracle would close his own eyes, too: he would concentrate, deep behind his eyelids, until his darkness embraced the darkness of his client. In this contact between shadows would be written the exact date of each one's passing.

Well, in Muitetecate, everyone had encouraged Adabo Salanje to consult the services of the diviner.

—*Go and you'll know the fateful day.*

Adabo refused. Go and find out his expiration date? So he could do what, exactly? Certain joys only come with not knowing. We don't learn how to live to suddenly end it all. Light doesn't accept its future: to be dust. We savour the luminescence of each laugh, the sumptuous flesh of love, the sweet shade of friendship—we don't bite off eternity bit by bit so we might soon be nothing, none, nobody.

Adabo Salanje got along well in this ignorance, this illusion of having no pact with time. Until one night he woke up shaking and sweating. Salanje was roused from his sleep in the pitch dark, his heart jumping through his pores. He'd dreamed he was in the house of the dead, where they'd asked him:

—*And you, Salanje, are you still dead?*

The spirits egged him on: he should make use of a consultation with the beyond to know when his second life would begin. After all, the later he found out, the earlier he would change states, the inverse of our logic here on this other side of the world.

The next day, stepping out onto the street, Salanje savoured the light as though for the first time. Could it be true, have I come from the beyond? Has my dream come to pass after all? Whether it had or hadn't, Adabo Salanje was rapt with all that blue, a warbling melody that gave the birds a new colour. At that same instant, he made up his mind and set off to consult the seer. He reflected on what his dream had taught him: if he knew the prior date of his posthumous death he could put one over on the calendar—death's advantage is surprise. Rob it of this edge, and eternal victory and vitality would belong to us, at present mere mortals.

So off he went. The oracle met him with a smug twist of his lips. He ordered the man to sit in the dark. The wise man took a peek at the time via the crosses he placed over Salanje's eyes. He required total silence. Suddenly, he confessed he was worried with a click of the tongue:

—*I can't do a thing. There's too much commotion going on in your head. Calm your thoughts down!*

Adabo was amazed. His immobility was complete. How was he to blame? The fortune-teller turned his focus again to his work. He would pull away the crosses and draw them closer again, as if he was having difficulty bringing things into focus.

—*You know something, sir? You've got a situation going on inside you...*

—*A situation?*

—*I'm not even sure how to tell you.*

Salanje swallowed his own throat. Were they not about to tell him his death was near, within a week's time? Would time be counted by the days he had left?

—*Am I going to die in next-to-no-time?*

—*No. You're not going to die.*

—*I'm not going to die? How am I not going to die?*

—*That's the problem.*

—*Give me an explanation for it, man!*

—*It's that you, Adabo Salanje, you're already dead.*

The client was gripped by a convulsion. After a few flies had flown past, he exploded into laughter. Nonsense! Having laughed so hard, he had to straighten up again to alleviate his ribs. Each time we burst into laughter, the number of our ribs multiplies exponentially. Therein lies the danger of hard, unhinged laughter. Adabo left the consultation, took a breath of fresh air, and then went back inside. He got off to a serious start:

—*So then do me the favour of explaining: what day was it, after all, that I died?*

—*Last night. You, sir, to tell the truth, are a newly deceased.*

Adabo misted over. Had it been the dream? Can death occur in lands misted over by dreams? He'd never heard of such a thing. A lie, the oracle must be lying. The guy was fooling around. Adabo's rage was such that he didn't know if he ought to laugh. He ended up letting his anger ferment:

—*All right then. So if I'm dead, as you have just said, I'm unable to pay for this appointment. I'll leave just like that.*

And he turned around and walked out. He didn't even want to know more. Something, though, had changed in the innermost part of his being. He began to feel ease at displaying kindness, patience with children, consideration toward the elderly. Women met his eyes with a new gentleness, they appeared to be almost diaphanous. He was no longer overtaken by an unrestrained fever in the face of their beauty. Above all, there was an even greater change: he no longer had access to the dreamworld. He, who had been an assiduous dreamer, would never again have visions.

The following morning, his wife woke him up with a bit of tenderness, a kiss on the forehead. Never before had he received such tenderness. And accompanied by a gentle sigh:

—*I missed you so much, Adabo!*

Lingering doubt seized him once again. Could he really be dead, as the other man had prophesied? Could his passing have been effected, and in effect, without his having been duly notified? Doubt burrowed deeper and deeper into him.

He didn't wait another minute. He went back to the the futurist. Arriving there, he halted for a second at the absence of people. An old chicken alone strutted in the vicinity. He knocked politely on the door but no one answered. He stepped into the dark room. When his eyes adjusted to the shadows he noticed the two ivory crosses, abandoned. He crouched down to pick them up and, before rising, still in a squat, he laid the ivory crosses over his eyelids. And waited for a sign. A voice frightened him:

—And *who are you, sir?*

—*I'm Adabo, I've come to see the oracle.*

—*You can't.*

—*I'll pay, up front even. In fact, the oracle owes me...*

—*You can't. The master has already passed.*

—*He died? When?*

He'd died the day before. So the master, as the other man called him, was incapable of predicting his own death? Adabo got a kick out of that. But the other man responded that

149

personal matters escape the powers even of wise men. Adabo turned to leave, gravity in every step: now, with the oracle dead, how could he determine the authenticity of his death?

—*Can I take these crucifixes?*

—*Take them, they're yours and then all's even.*

And he turned back to the road, hands in his pockets, ensuring that the little pieces of ivory were still there. The sun was already dipping low, the light's shipwreck stretching across the neighbourhood. At the bend of the corner, an illegible shadow made him feel afraid. He was covered in goosebumps when he recognized the voice of the seer:

—*I come in search of my ivory.*

He unpocketed the useless utensils and extended them in his cupped hands. Then, unexpectedly, he felt his hands immobilized, captive to the *feiticeiro*. At first, he fought back. Later, feeling the conviction of those other hands, he slackened his resistance. The diviner softened his voice, as if to extend an invitation:

—*Come with me.*

And as the two men made their way, they didn't leave a single footprint, as though they strode not across the sand but the clouds.

The Shadow's Departure

That morning, I rose at the crack of noon. My neighbour was nearly splitting the door in two. I answered: she didn't even ask please, and was already inside, crying all over my sofa.

—*It's my daughter, she's barely breathing.*

Her oldest daughter's asthma robbed her of peace. Entire nights the mother neglected sleep: administering essences, burning incense, invoking benedictions. But the danger would not fade. Her daughter, chest in her throat, gasped for air through the wide-open window. The girl had been like that ever since the sudden unsettling of her love affair, her heart fractured. Her beloved, once flesh and bone, had disappeared, swallowed up into never, vanished into smoky nothing. Where, when, how? Nothing, no one could say.

—*It's the times, as you know.*

The neighbour offered explanations with lucid ignorance. In our time, war grips so many nations. Who knows if the

young man fell into one of these pits war opens in the earth.
What's certain is that, ever since then, her daughter showed
no change, enfevered, huffing and puffing. Her soul had fled
from her mouth, but no breath came back through it. The
more she wheezed, the less she breathed. It wasn't only question of air: the girl was completely without atmosphere.

—*I don't know what to do with her, me...*

And what could I do? Poetry is no cure for those whom
life doesn't console. And the neighbour's distress was well-
founded: another attack and the girl would not survive. The
doctor told her so. But I was preparing to leave that same
afternoon. I showed her the tent, my sleeping bag, the equip-
ment. There was nothing she didn't already know:

—*I know you're going into the jungle. That's why I came.*

She wanted exactly this: that I bring back with me some
recommended plant, a miraculous thing, able to uncrucify
Jesus.

—*This one here, look closely, it has to be equal, exact, and
identical—no ands, no buts.*

I promised to deliver, I would come back equipped with
the miracle. She said goodbye with such pleading eyes that the
injustice wounded me: there are those, in this life, who have
such need of another's favour.

That afternoon, I waited for my guide, the man who
during the next few days would need to lead me through
agnostic landscapes. His reference letter read: Júlio Carlos

Alberto, former prisoner. The letter came from the director of the prison, on behalf of a friend. That I might give work to this newly free wrongdoer. Who knows if in the course of this work the mischief-maker wouldn't come to show more kindness?

The jailbird introduced himself, with tongue-twisted diction, in the slang of the streets:

—*I'm Julinho Casa'beto.*

He helped me wrap the tools needed for my trip. He went on about himself while he worked, full of words. He spoke of everything so as not to say a thing. He longed for conversation, revenge for the silences of the cell. He who loses all knows not what he wants. In this life, he who has the least loses the most.

It's this Julinho who, now, guides me through untamed forests groomed by nature alone. Because he remembers each obstacle, this guarantees his steady passage.

—*The day's nearly at an end.*

Yes, a short time from now, night will fall. We'll have trouble finding the oxcart driver who will deliver us to the house of the healer Nãozinha de Jesus. This woman was in my plans. She was the last of her kind: a doctor of healing plants. With her, I'd been earning an education. Nãozinha would circle shadows and pull up roots, tiny leaves, twigs. With these meagre materials she outduelled death. But the healer has a complaint: this vegetation is becoming scarce. These days, it barely hangs on to existence. And now, in a hollow in the woods, I wait for my body to faint as I gaze at the stars, the meteor showers. A short distance away, Julinho's elbow cuts this peaceful moment short.

—*Doctor, you'll excuse me: but what is it you're doing, horsing around in these jungles?*

—*It's my job, Júlio.*

—*But, Doctor: you're leaving the reserve to roam with wild herds? I guess each man digs his own hole. But tell me, I beg your pardon: have you ever seen a snake wear sandals?*

Pulling my blanket tight, I loosen my tongue. Overcome with fatigue, I dethread conversation: my occupation, the medicinal plants. This trip will, however, be the last. This work of mine can't continue. The monies were withdrawn, the entire thing was held to be of little importance. Priorities are elsewhere, they told me. What do you think you'll find there, in the illiterate jungle: the cure for AIDS? I didn't even respond. What argument could I make? There is, after all, another incurable ill: Acquired Humanodeficiency Syndrome. Inhuman sciences and occult scientists are never in short supply. What can I do to counteract them?

—*Forgive me, I hear you, but I don't follow you. It's only for a like of listening, I spent so long without a person's voice.*

I asked him to talk about himself, the reasons for his being thrown behind bars. What crime, after all, had occurred?

—I killed a man.

—And why did you do that?

—To take his moya *from him. There was a woman who asked me to do it.*

—To take his moya?

—Yeah, don't you know about moya? *It's a person's breath, his inner figure.*

I was familiar, but in another application. This man was not, after all, a common killer. He had not killed a man, but his shadow, the vessel that leads through other persons and times.

—It was a woman's request. She was almost dying.

—You liked this woman?

—She was my one and only passion.

Instead of causing annoyance, Julinho's conversation softened me. We fell asleep, the two of us, enveloped in the swirling smoke of the fire, beneath a starlit sky.

Next day, we set our course bright and early. We arrived soon after at the healer's place. We stayed sitting in the entrance of the *muti*, in accord with custom. In any African house worthy of the name, the day is spent outside the home, in the yard. There, children run round, chickens peck at the ground. Nãozinha takes some time to arrive. Finally, she makes her appearance. We greet each other in long, drawn-out rituals, hand in hand, touching bodies, trading souls. It was then that Nãozinha de Jesus noticed Julinho.

—You brought this one along?

She shuddered, bowing her head. The handle of her catan soared, with a whistle, through the airs. The blade stuck straight into the trunk of the sacred tree. The healer spit in the sap that dripped from the blow. She turned back to face the man, now with a victor's defiance. Julinho pulled away, downcast.

Then we sat. I owed her two words: explanation and request. I begin with the first subject: yes, that one, my final visit. My motives plunge Nãozinha into sadness. The healer is offended. I had promised her we would do combat together, both wishing to preserve her life-saving materials, to keep her age-old wisdoms in the world.

—*Now there's no more time. It's because they take everything from us, those who come from the city cut down everything, they don't leave us so much as a root...*

Still, I try for the light at the end of the tunnel. I say: If we go together, with the proper haste—Nãozinha's despondence cuts me short:

—*I no longer have any hereafter, my son. Why all the hurry?*

I move on to the second matter. I show her the bit of tiny plant I'm supposed to take back with me. I explain the urgency of the request, saving the life of the neighbour girl. The healer takes a look at the leaves and responds, disappointed:

—*These leaves, they've disappeared some time ago now, flew away, butterflying off somewhere.*

Not even a root, some leftover twig amid the brush? The healer purses her lips, in doubt. Only if it were somewhere in one last corner.

—*Come with me, help me look.*

Off we went, into the woods. Mist and leaves blocked the sun—it did me good, the cool air. A million enchantments distracted me. But beauties subtract from one another: we see the butterfly and forget the flower. Nãozinha stops in a clearing, sticks her hand out to say we've arrived. We both turn over the earth. Nothing, not even a trace of a plant. Even here, the traders have got to the plants first. Even here, they've dug, taken everything in wagon-loads to the city.

The next day, I return. If I'd left diminished, I was returning crushed.

How to explain to the neighbour that I hadn't brought the remedy? Is that something you explain to a mother? I entered through the side door with my head bowed. The woman let me in and, seeing me, dispensed with explanations. She took me by the hand to see her daughter's final pains. In the girl's room, we grew dizzy amid incense and essences. The girl was lying there on the bed and we could hear the air inside her, crackling like fire. The dying girl had lost her gaze: she peered at what wasn't there, landscapes of oblivion. Her eyes goaded me, magnetic. I was prisoner to their emptiness.

Suddenly, across that same fading face, a wry look spread. She fixed on someone who was entering the room. Who was she looking at, who had she recognized with such awe? I looked back in time to see the sharp gleam of a knife in a speeding fist. The very next second, the blade plunged into my chest. It stuck deep, a blow to the core. The last thing I saw was the asthmatic girl rise to hug my guide, Julinho Casa'beto. Then they bent down, the two of them together, to snatch my shadow.

Square of the Gods

———◆———

To Che Amur, whose version of these events served as the basis for this story.

1926: That was the year that marked the occasion. That's the year the personal story unfolded of the merchant Mohamed Pangi Patel, a powerful man who disbursed life and wealth on the Island of Mozambique. Accordingly, the years passed and Mohamed Pangi gave thanks to God for the beauty of the world and its marvels.

The Ismaelite grew rich off his own name, full of good cheer. His contentment only grew the day his only son came to tell him he'd decided to marry.

— *You know something, son? Life is a sweet perfume.*

Preparations for a wedding began. Such a celebration would never again be seen in such localities. Musicians came from Zanzibar, guests from Mombasa, peoples from Ibo and Angoche. The celebration lasted some thirty days. On every one of these days, the town square was covered with endless tables, boasting many a full spread. Day and night, foods of every variety and number could be found. The entire island turned up to help themselves by the belchful. In those days, not one of the poor felt the pang of hunger. And not a single family set foot in the kitchen: breakfast, lunch and dinner passed the day in the town square. While the many mouths opened wide to make way for such delights, Pangi stretched out over a bench, wise to the warm weather. His only occupation was to perspire as he basked in the joy of watching so many jaws at work.

—*But, Father, isn't this a bit much?*

Pangi's son began to worry about the mounting expenses. But Pangi responded with caution: *Better not a single bird in hand. Better to see great flocks spread their wings over the land. The heavens, after all, only came to be after the first bird's flight.* And he smiled:

—*Don't forget, son: life is a sweet perfume.*

And the old man began to explain: *We all carry this fragrance in our natural and congenital bodies. The fragrance, at first, bursts forth in all directions, strong, contagious. If anyone were to have smelled the world's first moment, they would have detected only their own perfume. But later, this fragrance thins. And then, in order to still sense it, people have to give their nostrils a workout: a headache for the nose. And that's how, from that point forward, with the smallest reminder of a shudder, even the surface of memories begins to evaporate...*

—*Father: how will we pay for all th*is?

The question was an appropriate one. It wasn't long before the creditors arrived, Pangi's houses were foreclosed upon. Later, the goods from his stores were sold at public auction. Pangi's endless properties grew ever more scarce. Once a rich man, he was demoted to a de-minted man, suit pockets full of sand. All of this, though, took place out of sight. No one beyond the dispossessed Pangi knew of this settling of accounts. Silent as a dagger, the Ismaelite went on sitting on his bench, in a state of pure fascination, as he gazed upon the endless celebration.

Tired of calling attention to the situation, the groom resolved to leave the island. That night, he gave his aging father an ultimatum: either the festivities came to an end or he'd turn his back on his old man forever. The old man smiled, astonishful, firmer than the firmament. He pointed to nothing at all, singled out among the square-dwellers a nothing-nobody. And then he spoke:

—*Listen to this song. I like this song so much it hurts me each time I listen to it.*

With gale-force rage, Pangi's son burst away with a mind to luggage, ships, and one-way trips. His bride held back, seated on the selfsame bench as Pangi. The young woman soaked in charm, eyes fixed on her father-in-law. She adjusted her wedding garments and stepped closer to the patriarch in the sunset of his life. She took hold of his hand and opened her big eyes wide:

—Father: would you dance this song with me?

The old man stood up without a word and allowed the bride to lead him to the middle of the square. There, the two danced together, on a floor of a thousand tiny lights, silver insects stirring up the dark. As he twirled round and round, the old man took in the scent of the jacarandas. Jealousy is what he felt, for the eternity of the trees' perfume.

—Tell me, my girl: do I still have my perfume?

She smiled without responding. Instead, she took him by the arm and brought him back to the dance. As they rocked back and forth, Mohamed Pangi whispered an apology. Didn't she know? All of this wasn't for them, the naive newlyweds, and their benefit. In the end, the quantity had been expended to celebrate other happenings. All through these days, the island put poverty behind it, not a single mother stood measuring her child's cries, the men drank not to forget but to taste the sweet sap of the waters of time.

—God must have loved to see a world like this. I'm offering this square up to Him, do you understand me?

And he took leave of the bride with a kiss on her forehead. *You have the scent of fruitfulness, my girl—only the earth's aroma is as sweet.*

—Tomorrow, in the wee hours, early in the morning, the festivities come to an end. Tell my son.

—Father, why don't you make your way home?

What home? The square was his home now. He would live in the very square he'd offered to the gods. The bride shook her handkerchief—farewell—through the air.

The next morning, dawn broke on the town square without any celebration. The banquet tables had disappeared, the band had left, dance shoes and dust surrendered to repose. All that remained was absence in disarray, mere memory of cheer and melodies. Alone on a park bench, Mohamed Pangi Patel remained motionless in an unexpected pose, with a strange smile. Was it God who smiled through his lips? Had his life been written off, a sort of last lien against his debts?

The bride was the first to reach his side. She knelt down next to the body and plucked from his hair the many distracted petals that had fallen from the towering trees. But later, as they carried his body, she went back to gathering handfuls of the fragrant petals and returning them to her father-in-law. Mohamed Pangi Patel departed the square and its jacarandas dusted with eternal life.

Translator's Acknowledgements

My deepest thanks go to Ammiel Alcalay, Esther Allen, and Maaza Mengiste, for their support and valuable advice during various stages of this project. And most of all, to Luisa Leme, who was often a first reader for these translations, and without whom this and many another endeavour would have been impossible.

About the Translator

Eric M. B. Becker is a writer, translator, and editor of *Words Without Borders*. His translations include work by Mia Couto, Carlos Drummond de Andrade, Lygia Fagundes Telles, and Djaimilia Pereira de Almeida. He has received grants and fellowships from the National Endowment for the Arts, Fulbright, and PEN America, and his work has appeared in *The New York Times*, *Freeman's*, *Foreign Policy*, and *World Literature Today*. He lives in New York City.